A
TASTE
OF
DAYLIGHT

my best efforts are
Alway for the children
And my best wishes are
to the Childrens Room
at the Library.
Sincerely
Crystal Thrasher

A
TASTE
OF
DAYLIGHT

Crystal Thrasher

A MARGARET K. MCELDERRY BOOK

Atheneum　　　*1984*　　　*New York*

Library of Congress Cataloging in Publication Data

Thrasher, Crystal.
   A taste of daylight.

   "A Margaret K. McElderry book."
   Summary: After her father dies, Seely and her family
move to the city where her mother feels life will be
easier, but life in the city presents a new set of
problems that the family has not encountered before.
   [1. Family life—Fiction.   2. City and town life—
Fiction.   3. Depressions—1929—Fiction]   I. Title.
PZ7.T4Tas   1984   [Fic]   84-2967
ISBN 0-689-50313-X

Published simultaneously in Canada by
   McClelland & Stewart, Ltd.
Composition by Maryland Linotype Composition Company
Baltimore, Maryland
Printed and bound by Fairfield Graphics
Fairfield, Pennsylvania
First Edition

NOTE OF THANKS

My thanks are long overdue to Fred
Mustard Stewart who introduced me to
Marilyn Marlow at Curtis Brown, Ltd.
And to Bonnie Bryant for taking my work
to Margaret McElderry at Atheneum Pub-
lishers, who is a rare kind of editor, a
wonderful person, and a true friend.

Crystal Thrasher

January 1984

DEDICATION

This book is for the boys who taught me to run a trapline, skin a rabbit, square dance, play a Jewsharp, and to get from one place to another without walking. My brothers: Ivan, Bill, Gene, and Doyle Knight. Love you guys.

In memory of another brother:
PARIS L. THRASHER
1907   1983

A
TASTE
OF
DAYLIGHT

chapter one

We had lived in Gus Tyson's house in the hills near Jubilee longer than we had stayed anywhere else. I'd hoped that we could stay until I finished high school. But after Dad died and Mom started selling her pies to the hotel in Bedford, she had lost no time finding a place there for us to live.

In August, Mom rented the old carriage house that sat at the rear of Elvira Spragg's big stone house, and we moved to the city. Gus Tyson hauled the household furnishings on his flatbed logging truck, taking my brother Robert with him. Gus's sister, Fanny Phillips, carried Mom and me to our new home in her automobile.

3

The car had no more than passed the city limits when Mom said, "I've finally made it out of the hills and hollows to where I can see daylight." She shook her head as if she still couldn't believe it. "I never thought I'd live to see the day," she added.

"Zel, I hope the day never comes when you regret it," Fanny replied quietly.

Every time she and Fanny Phillips got home from delivering Mom's pies to the hotel, Mom would relate some new advantage that she said we could look forward to when we lived in the city.

"I'll be doing my baking at the hotel once we're settled in the Spragg house," she said. "No more standing over a hot stove all day to make a dozen pies. They have ovens there that will hold that many pies at one time."

Robert looked at me and raised his eyebrows as if to say, "Do they?" but neither one of us contradicted her. We had heard so many times how much bigger and better everything was in Bedford that we had begun to discount a lot of it as wishful thinking on Mom's part.

Mom had the notion that once we were out of the rocky hills of Greene County we would be on easy street. To hear her tell it, Robert and I would never want for a thing.

I thought of what Fanny Phillips had just said, and I prayed that Mom would never have reason to regret this move.

The house that Mom had rented had a high, hipped roof that sloped down to meet faded gray-painted weatherboard, and the weatherboard ran to the streaked-gray limestone slab walls. Attached at one end of the

4

house was a lean-to shed that had never seen a coat of paint.

The inside consisted of one large, high-ceilinged room, which stretched nearly the length of the house, with a door at each end. One door led into a small room, and beyond it was the kitchen. Above the small room and the kitchen area was an open loft room. Steps as narrow as a stepladder rose to the loft from the kitchen.

Since Robert and I had always shared a room, I assumed that we would sleep in the loft. But Mom said that Robert could sleep on the daybed downstairs. She was afraid he might walk in his sleep and fall from the open balcony.

After the thought had entered her head, Mom couldn't leave it alone. She had Gus Tyson string clothesline from the post at the head of the stairs to the other side of the loft, closing in the balcony, even though Robert wouldn't be sleeping up there.

It was late in the afternoon and the house was hotter than a bake oven when Mom finally called a halt to the laying of carpet and placing of furniture. "It's time for a bite to eat and a cup of coffee," she said. She sent Robert to the shed for wood to make a fire in the cookstove.

Robert came back empty-handed. "There's no wood out there," he said, his face a picture of mystification.

Mom seemed as puzzled as Robert. "No wood?"

"Zel, it's too hot for coffee," Fanny Phillips said. "I'd settle for lemonade and peanut butter sandwiches with the young'uns."

Mom wasn't happy about it, but that's what they

5

had. She couldn't get over the fact that there was no firewood at hand, and she harped on it all the while we were eating. There had always been plenty for the gathering in Greene County.

"Zel, I've got a truckload of scrap lumber piled up around the sawmill," Gus Tyson said. "I'll bring it to you tomorrow."

"I didn't allow to be buying wood," Mom replied.

"No charge, Zel," Gus said, wiping the sweat from his face. "We'll just call it a housewarming gift."

Gus and Fanny left soon after we finished eating. Gus said he had work to do at the sawmill, and Fanny Phillips said she had to get ready for church that evening. But I figured they were getting out to where they could find a cool breeze and a breath of fresh air.

I wished for an excuse to get out of the house and look over the new neighborhood, and almost immediately the wish was granted.

"Seely," Mom said, "why don't you take Robert and go look for stovewood? Gus Tyson said there should be something along the old Bottom Road, there at the end of the alley."

Robert picked up a small basket, and we went down the kitchen steps into the lean-to shed and from it out to the alley.

"Seely, that's not much of a house, is it?" Robert observed quietly.

"No, it's not," I replied. "But as long as Mom is pleased with it, we can't complain."

The house would shelter us and hold the weather at bay, and that was about all anybody could ask of a

6

house. Besides that, I thought, for the first time in my life I'd have a room of my own. It didn't matter to me that the room was wide open. I could read and write and even talk to myself, with no fear of someone asking what I was doing.

"The only drawback that I can see to the place," I told Robert, "it's way too close to the other houses."

Robert kind of smiled. "I think you just miss the hills and trees we had in Jubilee."

It wasn't as though the city didn't have hills and trees, I told him. But the hills were topped with tall limestone buildings and concrete streets, and the trees grew beside cement sidewalks. The way I looked at it, that was a far cry from the hills we knew that were crowned with tall trees, where we could feel the soft earth beneath our feet.

"Finding firewood was a lot easier in the woods too," Robert said, scrounging along the edge of Bottom Road for twigs.

Bottom Road wasn't much more than an alley itself, only a little bit wider and spread with limestone dust and fine gravel instead of cinder clinkers and wood ashes. Straggly trees grew along the roadside, and far ahead of us, where the road fell out of sight over a hill, we could see a good stand of timber.

"Let's go to yonder woods," Robert said, "and see what lies over the hill."

We had come quite a ways from home, and the sun was getting low. "It will be dark soon," I said. "And Mom will be looking for us. We can fill the basket with broken-off branches from these trees." I motioned for

7

Robert to follow me, as I waded into the high weeds and toward the nearest tree.

We soon had the basket full, but Robert wanted one more branch for good measure. Just as he stepped on one end to break it, someone hollered, "Hey, what are you doing?"

The branch snapped with a loud crack, and we both turned quickly to face the road. A boy and girl about my age stood there watching us.

"What are you kids doing?"

"What does it look like I'm doing?" Robert replied sharply.

They looked at the ground, then lifted their eyes and stared at us some more.

"You startled us," I said. "We didn't know there was anyone else within a mile of here."

The girl smiled. The boy never once glanced my way. He kept his eyes on Robert. I picked up the basket and went to the road.

"We moved into Mrs. Spragg's carriage house today," I babbled on. "And we forgot to bring wood for the cookstove. That's what we're doing now," I waved my hand toward Robert. "We're gathering firewood."

Idiot! I thought to myself. Why can't you ever keep your mouth shut.

The girl was still smiling. "We live just over the hill yonder," she said. "You come ahead to our house, and Grandpa Hollis will give you all the firewood you can use." She looked at the basket of broken twigs and branches. "That makes good kindling," she said, "but it won't hold heat for cooking."

"It will last as long as we want it," Robert muttered.

8

Then to me, he said, "Come on, Seely. We've got to get home."

He struck off up the road, looking neither to the left nor right and walking fast.

"We'll get wood from the mill tomorrow," I said, starting after Robert. "But thanks for the offer anyway."

She waved her hand and they went on down the road.

"Why did you have to talk to them kids?" Robert asked, when I had caught up with him.

"They seemed friendly to me," I said. "They didn't mean to frighten us."

"I wasn't scared. That old tree didn't belong to them."

"We don't know, Robert. Maybe it did."

It had been after eight, but not yet dark, when I went to the loft room and got ready for bed. That was hours ago, and I still wasn't asleep. Even with both windows open, it was hot and stuffy in the loft. I thought if there was a breeze stirring I would get a cross-draft from the windows. But not one breath of air passed by my bed.

"Seely," Robert whispered from the top of the stairs. "Are you asleep?"

I whispered, "No."

"I can't sleep," he said. "Would you like me to bring my pillow and sleep up here with you? I could put a blanket on the floor," he coaxed.

"Robert, go back to bed before you wake Mom. She expects to find us in our own beds in the morning and that's where we'd better be. If we want to keep peace in this house," I added under my breath.

He gave a long, exaggerated sigh, then a moment later he whispered goodnight from the foot of the stairs.

9

chapter two

Robert was sound asleep on the daybed, and Mom had already gone to work when I awoke the next morning. Mom had left for work without having her morning coffee, so the kitchen was cool. Mom had put a note on the kitchen table for Robert and me, telling us to clean the junk from the lean-to shed the first thing. Gus Tyson would need a place to stack the firewood when he got here.

I called Robert, then I got the milk out of the ancient refrigerator that came with the house, and we had cold cereal and milk for our breakfast. We ate, though Robert grumbled a lot at the work ahead. Then we started clearing the shed of its accumulation of trash.

Robert had an old automobile tire in each hand. "What are we supposed to do with this junk?"

"Just get it out of the lean-to," I answered. "Mom can decide what's to be done with it later."

I was sweeping the hard-packed dirt floor of the lean-to when Elivra Spragg walked in through the dust. I stopped sweeping and started fanning the air with my hand.

"Don't let me stop you," she said. "I just came down to tell you to put this trash by the alley. Pete Elwood will pick it up and haul it away for fifty cents a month."

Mrs. Spragg peered into every corner of the shed, nodded to me, and went away.

"I wonder what Mom will say when she hears that she has to pay a man to carry off the trash."

Robert kind of grinned and shook his head. "She'll raise the devil," he said. "But she should know by now that a place in the city is different from Jubilee."

Early in the afternoon Gus Tyson arrived with a truck full of scrap lumber from his sawmill. Robert and I helped him unload and stack the firewood.

As Gus was leaving, he said, "Give me a hand with that junk, and I'll haul it to the dump. Your mom wouldn't like to see that unsightly mess in her yard."

Robert allowed that Gus was right. So when Gus Tyson left, he took the trash with him. That solved our trash problem—at least for a little while.

Robert and I went into the house to clean off the dust and dirt. Only cold water came out of the faucet over the sink. Robert said that we might as well have washed at the pump outside. We learned later it would have been cheaper because we had to pay for water we used in the house.

It was after five o'clock when Mom got home from work. I had supper ready, and I'd let the fire die out in the cookstove so the kitchen would be a little cooler for eating in.

"I didn't expect to be at that hotel the livelong day," Mom said. "But when I'd finished with the baking, the proprietor put me to work helping the chef. He said that would be my job from now on," she added.

"You won't have to do that every day, will you?" Robert asked.

Mom nodded her head. "Six days a week," she said. "Maybe seven, if I can get the work. I don't like to leave you kids here alone," she added, "but if I'm to make a living for us, I'll need to work every hour I can get."

"Don't worry about Robert and me," I said. "We can look after ourselves."

"Seely, you don't know the first thing about city life," Mom said. "Anything can happen. I want you to stay here at home, keep the doors locked, and don't let strangers into the house while I'm at work."

I started to tell her that we'd be fine here alone, but she cut me off to say, "Don't argue with me, Seely. And mind what I tell you for once."

Robert's eyes met mine, and he barely moved his head, cautioning me to be quiet. Then he turned to Mom with a wide smile. "Would you like to see the shed?" he asked her. "We've got it cleaned, and we've racked up the wood that Gus Tyson brought us."

12

Robert got up from the table, Mom slid her chair back and went outside with him to look at the shed. I carried the supper dishes from the table to the sink, then I followed them.

I remarked that it was surprisingly cool in the shed, when it had been so hot all day, and Mom said it was the dirt flood that kept it cool. "It will probably be warm in here this winter," she added.

Mom glanced out the shed door, then took a longer look in every direction. "What did you do with all the junk that was in here?" she asked.

"We loaded it onto Gus Tyson's truck," Robert replied. "And he hauled it to the dump."

Mom nodded her head as if to say she had expected as much.

"Mrs. Spragg told me when I rented this house that I would have to pay Pete Elwood fifty cents to have the trash picked up."

Robert and I looked at each other, then at Mom. "She told Seely and me the same thing," Robert said.

As we were getting ready to go to bed that night, Mom brought up again her uneasiness about leaving Robert and me alone while she was working. I reminded her that school would be starting soon. We would only be alone for a few hours a day.

"Why, that's right," Mom said. "I'd almost forgotten it was nearly school time again. Where did the summer go?" she asked of the air around her. "Seems like yesterday . . ." She stopped and didn't finish her thought.

Though she didn't say, I knew what Mom meant. The days of summer had been long and hot, the work and the light of day never ending. Yet the weeks and months seemed to have flown like the darkness before the dawn, bringing the end of summer before we were aware of its passing.

Mom smiled at me as if we had come to an understanding, for the first time in our lives.

"When you are ready for bed, Seely, check the doors and turn out the lights. I'm going to bed now."

And she did.

I took that to mean I could stay up as long as I liked. I could do as I pleased until I wanted to go to bed. I went to the front of the house to check the door. Robert was sound asleep on the daybed. Suddenly, I was so tired and sleepy that I couldn't keep my eyes open. I checked the kitchen door, turned out the lights, and climbed up the ladder steps to my bed.

chapter three

A day or two later, Robert and I started out to find the schoolhouse. He wanted to see it before school began. Just as we got to the end of the alley, Elvira Spragg came out of her house and stopped us.

"Now that you are caught up with the work down there," she said, "I wonder would you come up here and help me clean my cellar?" She looked straight at Robert and added, "Later, I'll need someone to dig the onions and potatoes out of my garden and store them away for me."

Robert opened his mouth to answer her, but she didn't give him a chance to say a word.

15

"I'm getting too old to stoop and dig and lug stuff to the cellar," she said. "But it would pose no hardship for a young'un like you, if you were of a mind to work," she added.

"I'd be pleased to do it for you," Robert said.

Mrs. Spragg favored Robert with a smile. "There will be a little something for you," she said. "Mr. Spragg was a big man at the stone mill, and he left me comfortably well off when he died. But I can't be comfortable knowing the work's not being done."

I thought that even though Mr. Spragg had had a lot of money, you couldn't tell it by looking at his widow. Time or hard work or both had worn her away till she was all bones and sharp angles, covered by a cotton housedress.

While I studied Elvira Spragg, she was eyeing me. "I could use a girl's help in the house," she said, "if your mother could spare you."

I said that I would ask Mom about it and let her know.

She nodded her head. "Well, I won't keep you from your errand," she said.

"We're not going on an errand," Robert told her. "We're looking for the schoolhouse."

"The grade school sits on the corner of Oak and Fourteenth Street," Mrs. Spragg said. "And you can see the high school from there."

We thanked her and went on our way. She was still standing by the alley when we turned the corner on Maple Street.

Robert usually talked a mile a minute when we were together, but he hadn't said a word since we left Mrs.

Spragg. I guess he was thinking of all the work he had gotten himself into. It would not be easy, cleaning the cellar and getting the vegetables out of the ground.

"Mrs. Spragg said there'd be a little something for us," Robert said. "Do you think she aims to pay me for helping her?"

"Robert, I don't think Mom would allow you to take money for helping an old woman."

"But what if the old woman was rich, and she wanted to give me money?" he persisted. "Would I have to turn it down?"

"I wouldn't count on getting any money," I told him. "Then you won't be disappointed when she thanks you nicely and gives you a cookie."

Robert didn't say any more about it, but his talk of money was catching. I found myself thinking of all the things we could buy, if we got paid for our work. In my head I figured the cost of pencils and paper for school, including a loose-leaf notebook for me. If Mrs. Spragg gave us as much as a dollar, we could buy it ourselves.

We found the grade school right where Mrs. Spragg had said it would be. It was a three-storied, square limestone building, bigger than the high school I had gone to last year in Oolitic. Robert stared wide-eyed and open-mouthed at the size of it.

"Seely, I wish we hadn't found this school," he said finally. "Now I'll have nightmares about finding my way around inside it."

"It won't seem so big after a few days," I said.

I pointed on down the street to where the high school seemed to cover one whole city block. "Look at the size of that place," I told Robert. "And I've got to find class-rooms in there."

"Yeah, but you're grown up," he retorted. "I'm only ten years old and in fourth grade."

"Phooey!" I said shortly. "You're almost as tall as I am."

Robert got quiet and moved away from me.

I shouldn't have belittled his fears. I knew how he was feeling. I had been ten years old, and scared to death, when I'd walked into that strange little one-room school in Greene County. And I hadn't been alone like Robert. I'd had my brother Jamie there beside me. A strange school could be frightening, even for the bravest. To a young boy from the hills, it could be a belly-shattering experience.

"You'll make new friends the very first day," I said gently. "And after that, you'll like going to school."

"You think so?" he asked hopefully.

I nodded. "I'm sure of it."

Robert brightened up right away. Now that we had found the school, he wanted to walk downtown and look around. "While we are this close," he said, "we ought to know what it's like."

I hesitated. My sense of direction wasn't to be trusted. I could get lost in the pocket of a shirt. But Robert wanted badly to venture into the city.

As if he knew why I was hesitating, Robert said, "We've got all day. Besides, I won't let you get lost."

"All right," I said at last. "But I don't want to hear you complain about being tired."

We walked up one concrete hill and down another, heading toward the main part of the city. The courthouse and the stores around the square sat on the only flat surface we had seen anywhere.

There were a lot of stores that had gone out of business, and empty-faced men sat in the doorways, leaning against the buildings. They had no more business than the closed stores, I told Robert. They were killing time, waiting for work to come to them.

"They may have a long wait," Robert said.

We hurried by the vacant buildings and stopped to look in the windows at the Woolworth's Five and Dime store. But we didn't go inside. We didn't have the five or dime to spend.

I wanted to go home. I had seen all I wanted to see of the city. But I couldn't find Maple Street. I read the street signs as we walked by them. The names of trees had given way to numbers.

As soon as I knew I was lost, I could feel the hot pavement through the soles of my shoes, twice as hot as before. My feet started hurting. I was hungry and tired and ready to sit on the curb and cry.

"Robert, have you seen any sign of Maple Street?"

"I haven't been looking for it," he replied. "I figured to cross the railroad track and go back the way we came from the schoolhouse." He grinned impishly. "We've got to be sure I can find my way home from school every day," he added.

As we went down the alley to the house at last, Elvira Spragg was in her garden, picking bell peppers and dropping them into her gathered apron. "You've been gone a long while," she said. "Did you have any trouble finding the school?"

"We found it right where you said it would be," Robert replied.

She waited as if expecting us to tell her where else we had been, but we kept on going.

"She doesn't need to know that we went downtown," Robert whispered.

"We'd better not tell Mom either," I said quietly. "She would lock us in the house and take the key with her to work."

The first thing we did after we got in was to take off our shoes and count the blisters on our feet. We had gone barefoot all summer, except for church on Sundays and the day we had moved here. Even though Mom said that we had to wear shoes all the time now that we were living in the city, today was the first time we'd put them on since we got here.

"Seely, I've been wondering about something." Robert lowered his head to study the blisters on his feet. "Until last year, Dad bought us new shoes and things to start school with. But now that Dad isn't here, do you think we'll still get new shoes?"

I told him that I didn't know. Everything was different now. "But we mustn't ask Mom for anything," I said. "She will give us whatever she can, and we'll make do with what we've got."

Robert sat rubbing his feet as if that was all he had on his mind. Then he said, "With Julie teaching school up north, if she knew we needed it, she might send Mom money to help out."

"Julie isn't obligated to us for anything," I replied shortly. "Just because she's our sister, it doesn't necessarily mean that she should help us. Nobody helped her," I added under my breath.

Julie had worked two jobs to pay her own way through teacher's college. She had been home only twice since she went away to school, once for Christmas, then again a few months later when we had buried Dad.

But Julie wrote to us. Not much, just a postcard now and then. And I answered her cards with long letters, telling her all the good things. I had never let on to Julie that we were having a hard time, and I wouldn't do it now.

I didn't know how much the thirty cents an hour that the hotel paid Mom would add up to on payday, but I was almost sure it wouldn't be enough to buy firewood and groceries and cover all the bills. If we were to make it through the winter, Robert and I would have to find a way to make some money.

"Seely, are you mad at me about something?"

I shook my head. "I was just thinking," I said. I pulled my bare feet onto the chair under me and leaned across the table toward Robert. "I was thinking how well the two of us work together. And I've got a good notion how to make more money this winter."

"What do you figure to do?"

"Work for Mrs. Spragg," I said. "Both of us." I paused and took a deep breath. If Robert was going to give me an argument, this would be the time for it. "Robert, I'm not going to ask Mom about working for Mrs. Spragg. And you mustn't either. You're the one who reminded me that she could afford to pay us. In the morning you and I are going to ask Mrs. Spragg how much she is figuring to pay for the work at her house."

"Ask her for money?" Robert was horrified. "Seely, we can't do that. Mom would kill us!"

"Not if she doesn't know it," I said. "And who's to tell her?"

"Not me," Robert said, scooting off his chair and heading for the door. "I'm not going to open my mouth!"

chapter four

We had supper ready when Mom got home from work that evening, and the house was neat and clean. Far as I could tell, there was nothing left undone.

Robert met her at the front door and walked to the kitchen with her. "Supper is ready for you," he said.

Mom gave him a tired smile and took her place at the kitchen table.

"Don't wait supper for me tomorrow night," Mom said. "Bad as I hate to spend the money, I have to buy shoes and uniforms to work in. Nedra Noyer, a woman who works at the hotel, said that she would take me to the store where she does all her shopping. It's the only one in town she can afford," Mom added. "Nedra has four young'uns in school to buy for."

I poured a cup of coffee and set it in front of Mom. "We saw Mrs. Spragg this morning and she told us how to find the school."

"I take it that you kids had to go see it for yourselves." Mom turned to look at me. I nodded my head yes.

"It's not as far as Robert had to walk to school in Jubilee," I said. "And the high school is nearby. We can walk back and forth to school together."

Mom mumbled something about being thankful for small favors, and she didn't say a word about Robert and me leaving the house.

As we ate supper Mom talked about her job at the hotel and the other women who worked there. Most of them were widows, Mom said, or else their man had walked out and left them with the children to raise by themselves.

"About all the women bring their own brown paper bags to work with them," Mom said. "And when they leave in the evening, the bags are filled with rolls and the meat that comes back on plates from the dining room. I see it every day and I thank God that I'm not that hard up yet."

Hearing this made me wonder more than ever if Mom's paycheck would stretch far enough to cover our living expenses. If the other women who worked at the hotel couldn't make a living there, it stood to reason Mom couldn't either. It looked to me like Mom, in her eagerness to be out of the hills, had bitten off more than she could comfortably chew.

But if Mrs. Spragg would pay Robert and me for working, and if we could find other jobs that we could do after school, we might make enough money to tide us over until spring. I'd do anything, I told myself, as long as I knew it would keep Mom from having to bring home a paper bag of scraps to feed us.

After supper, Mom took a basin of warm water and went to her room. To sponge herself, she said, as she closed the door.

"Seely," Robert whispered while we were washing the dishes. "How much money do you think Mrs. Spragg will give us?"

I said, "Sh-sh," and shook my head to silence him. This was no time to be talking about money from Mrs. Spragg. Mom might come in and hear us. Then the fat would be in the fire for sure. It was one thing to do something without first asking Mom, but another thing entirely to go ahead and do it after she had told us not to.

When Robert went to the lean-to to get wood and fill the box for the next morning, I went with him. "We'll not talk about Mrs. Spragg while Mom is in the house," I told him. "We can't risk having her hear us. She might forbid us even to go up there, let alone work for Mrs. Spragg."

We filled the water reservoir on the stove to make sure there would be warm water whenever Mom needed it and carried the day's garbage to the can out by the alley. Then we walked to Bottom Road and back, bored to death with this place where we knew no one and there was nothing to do.

We turned the light on over the kitchen table and got

out the checkerboard. For once, Robert didn't even try to win.

Mom called from her room and asked what we were doing. "You're awfully quiet in there," she said.

"I was just thinking of going to the toilet," Robert answered, trying to be smart-alecky.

"Then go on," Mom said, "and get it over. Then you can lock the doors and go to bed," she added.

We took turns running down the dark path to the little shanty that was hidden among the shrubs and vines at the back of the lot. Then Robert locked the doors. He waited until I had a lamp lighted in the loft room, the only place in the house where there wasn't electricity. Then he turned out the light in the kitchen and went to bed.

A while back, Julie had sent me a five-year diary. I tried to write in it every day. Sometimes, I would run over the lines allotted to the day and end in the next year. But tonight, when I finished writing, I had space left over. It doesn't take much room to write, "I hope Mrs. Spragg offers to pay Robert and me for our work, then I won't have to ask her to."

I turned the lamp down low, then I blew out the light and went to bed. But not to sleep. My mind kept going round and round, thinking of ways to earn money. There had to be people in this city who would hire me to work for them. But first, I would try Mrs. Spragg. More than likely she would take it for granted that I had talked to Mom or I wouldn't be there. And I aimed to be there, ready for work, first thing in the morning.

I was stirring the pancake batter for breakfast when

Robert came to the kitchen wearing the raggedest shirt and overalls I had ever seen. "I dug these out of the patching bag last night," he said. "I figured someone cleaning cellars ought to look like he can use the money."

I smiled at him and held out my skirt to show him that I was wearing the oldest dress that I could find.

Mom would have a fit if she saw us dressed like this. But I figured we would be done with the cellar and back home in plenty of time to change our clothes. And Mom would be late because she was going shopping this evening. That would give us more than enough time to get home before she did.

With every step up the alley, I rehearsed how I would tell Elvira Spragg that if we worked for her she would have to pay us. Yet when she opened the door and asked us in, I didn't open my mouth.

"Well, looks to be a good day to clean the cellar," Mrs. Spragg said, glancing at the gray, overcast sky. "It doesn't look like a fit day for anything else."

Mrs. Spragg led the way to the cellar door, pushed a button, and a dim light went on down there. Even on a bright, sunny day that cellar would have been a deep, dark hole. But on this gray, sunless morning it was like a dungeon.

Robert took one look down the cellar steps, then he turned to me. "Seely?"

I don't know if I reached for Robert's hand, or if he sought mine, but suddenly our hands were clasped tightly together.

"The boy can do the work by himself," Mrs. Spragg

said. "He can find the cleaning things down there. He don't need his sister to hold his hand while he does it," she added.

I knew that I would go down those cellar steps with Robert, or we would leave this house and go home. Elvira Spragg didn't have money enough to pay me to leave him alone in that place.

"My brother and I work together," I said, daring her to deny me the right.

I could tell by the way she closed her face to me she didn't like it. But all she said was, "Carry the junk at the foot of the stairs to the trash pile as you go home." Then she closed the cellar door in my face.

Wide wooden planks served as steps to the cellar, but the walls and floor of the room were stone slabs. Plank shelves lined one wall, and wooden vegetable bins sat on the floor beneath them. An ancient washing machine and concrete rinse tub were shoved snug to the far wall, and a water spigot stuck out of the stone above them. I turned the faucet and water gushed out in noisy spurts.

I found the soap powder and scrub brushes, and Robert brought a ladder from the dark recesses by the furnace. He set the ladder at one end of the shelves so I could reach the top one, then he went to the other end of the bins and started cleaning them.

Almost at once, we realized we would need a big box for the dirty shelf paper and the straw from the bins. While I was searching the other end of the cellar, I came upon a set of steps topped with double doors leading to the outside. I called Robert and showed him what I had found.

"If we can get those doors open," he said. "We could carry off the trash and never step foot in her kitchen."

After about three tries, Robert took a deep breath and said, "Heave ho!" And with that last shove, one of the doors flopped open and fell to the ground with a loud crash.

I expected to hear Elvira Spragg yelling at us, or see her at the open door. But she never bothered us at all.

The light from the doorway was dim and gray, like the sky, but it was a sight better than the dark shadows that had filled the cellar. I told Robert that I didn't feel so much like a mole in a hole, now that the outside door was open.

We finished scrubbing the shelves and bins. Then, while Robert carried trash to the dumping spot, I wrapped a rag around the broom and wiped the cobwebs from the walls and ceiling.

"Not much left to do now," I told Robert, when he came back inside. "We have to take her junk from the foot of the stairs, then we'll be done."

Robert looked at the floor. Then as his eyes came up to meet mine, he grinned sheepishly. "Seely, do you know what we forgot to do?"

I looked around the cellar. I didn't see anything we had forgotten to do.

"We forgot to ask Mrs. Spragg how much money she aimed to pay us for this work," he said.

I laughed and sat down on the bottom step of the stairs. Robert sat down beside me. But he wasn't laughing. "What if she doesn't pay us at all?" he said. "I'll bet you wouldn't think that was funny."

29

I told him that I was laughing at us. "We are so green," I said. "Without her offering us one red cent, Elvira Spragg has gotten her cellar rid up from top to bottom."

"The Reverend Mister Paully used to say that the laborer was worthy of his hire," Robert quoted.

"I'm not even sure we were hired," I said. "Maybe we volunteered."

I got up to sort through the junk at my feet, tossing things left and right into the trash box. I put to one side a small straight-backed child's chair. It was well built and solid, just the right size to fit under a window in my loft room. I thought since Mrs. Spragg was throwing it away, I might as well take it.

Robert had found an old red railroad lantern in the junk. He raised and lowered the glass globe, turned the lantern upside down to see if it leaked. Satisfied that it was in working condition, he put it with the small chair.

Surely Mrs. Spragg couldn't object to us taking these things, I told Robert when he asked if we were stealing them. "She was throwing them away," I said. "But to make you feel better I'll ask Mrs. Spragg if we can have them."

We carried everything else outside, then closed the cellar door and fastened it back the way we had found it.

"We had better go now, Seely," Robert said. "Mom will be home before we can get cleaned up."

I was ready to quit. But the windows weren't washed, and the floor needed scrubbing. "I guess we can finish this in the morning," I said.

We were washing our hands when the door to the

kitchen opened, and Mrs. Spragg called, "You kids come on up. Your mother is here waiting for you."

Mrs. Spragg went away, but she left the door open. After a moment, I could hear the murmur of voices from the kitchen, but not what they were saying.

"I wonder why Mom didn't go after her work shoes," I said.

"I don't know," Robert said. "But I know there will be the devil to pay when she gets us home."

"You'd better believe it," I replied.

I picked up the chair and started up the stairs. "Don't forget your lantern," I told Robert.

I didn't have to ask for the chair and lantern. When Mrs. Spragg saw them in our hands, she gave them to us.

After I had thanked her, and we were leaving, Robert said, "We didn't get done, but we'll be back tomorrow to finish it for you."

She waved her hand as if to say it was of no importance.

Mom didn't say a word on the way home. Robert walked on one side of her, swinging the old lantern, and I was on the other carrying the chair. She set a fast pace for a tired woman, I thought, as we hurried to keep up with her. But I knew from past experience that when Mom was angry she could move swifter than a river rushing downhill.

Robert went around the house to the lean-to with his lantern, but I followed Mom through the front door, taking the chair with me.

"Get that thing out of the house," Mom said. "And keep it out!"

31

I opened the kitchen door and set the chair in the shed.

"Elvira Spragg stopped me and said that you two had been working there all day," Mom said, as she shoved kindling into the cookstove to start the supper fire. "She should have paid you in cash money instead of that junk nobody can use."

"We can use the lantern," Robert said. "It will come in handy for lighting the path to the outhouse."

"Just what we need," Mom snapped. "A red light hanging over our privy for all to see."

Robert mumbled that we needed more kindling, and he left the room, leaving me to take the brunt of Mom's anger and to pacify her if possible.

"You kids finish that cellar tomorrow, like you promised," Mom said. "Then let that be the last of it."

I put the plates on the table and turned toward Mom. "Mrs. Spragg has asked me to work after school, when my chores here are done. And she wants Robert to get in the garden stuff for her. He has already told her he'll do it," I added.

Robert had come in while I was speaking to Mom.

Mom looked at Robert and me, her face thoughtful. But there seemed to be a trace of new hope in her eyes. "Do you kids want to work for Elvira Spragg?"

We both nodded and said yes at the same time.

"Then I've no objection," Mom said. "But there will have to be an understanding about your wages."

Robert looked my way, we both smiled, then I went on setting the table for supper.

"I'll just speak to Elvira myself," Mom said firmly. "Then there will be no question about it."

That ended Mom's talking to Robert and me about what we had done today. Later that night I asked her why she hadn't gone to buy new shoes. She said that Nedra Noyer had to work overtime and she couldn't find the store by herself. They would do their trading after payday, when they would both have money on hand.

chapter five

Mom didn't eat much early in the morning, but she did like a little something with her coffee. This morning, I got up early to make pancake batter, enough for Robert and me later, and put one in the oven to bake. When Mom came to the kitchen dressed for work, I had the coffee poured and her breakfast on the table. Though I didn't always get up when Mom left for work, some mornings I liked to have her coffee ready for her.

She ate with one eye on her coffee cup and the other one on the clock. I could keep her cup filled, but I couldn't do a thing about the time. At five o'clock Mom left.

"It looks like it will be a pretty day," she said, as she stepped out the door. "Maybe you should do the washing when you get done at the Spragg place." Then as an afterthought she added, "Just do the things you and Robert will need for school."

I locked the front door after Mom, then I went to the loft room to sort through my school clothes. There weren't many. I rolled them into a bundle, blew out the light, and went downstairs to sort Robert's things.

When Robert came to the kitchen a while later, the galvanized washtub full of water was heating on the cookstove for the laundry. He rubbed the sleep from his eyes, looked at the tub of water and the clothes. "Seely, we can't do a washing today. We've got to finish that cellar."

"We'll do the laundry first," I told him. "Then while the clothes are drying on the line, we'll go to Mrs. Spragg's."

Robert gave me a sleepy grin. "I didn't feel much like facing that cellar first thing this morning anyway," he said.

By ten thirty, we had had our breakfast, the house-work was done, and the clothes were starched and drying on the line. Another tub of water was heating on the cookstove for Robert and me to take a bath when we got home from Mrs. Spragg's.

"I wasn't looking to see you here," she greeted us. "I saw you hanging out the wash."

"It wasn't much," I replied. "Only a few things we needed freshened up for school."

"We'd like to get the cellar done," Robert said. "We

35

don't have many days like this one, when we've got nothing to do."

I gave him a mean look, but he didn't seem to see it.

"Then you'd better light into it," Mrs. Spragg told him.

She pushed the button that lighted up the cellar and cautioned us to watch our step. Then she closed the door firmly behind us.

"As if she was afraid a mouse or spider would get to her," Robert whispered.

I went at once to fill the concrete tub with hot soapy water. "I'll scrub the floor," I told Robert. "And you can wash the windows."

Suddenly the wide cellar door flew open and hit the ground outside. Startled, I turned to see Mrs. Spragg at the top of the steps peering down on us. She watched as Robert placed the ladder under a window and picked up the bucket of sudsy water. Then she called to him.

"Son, leave the cleaning to your sister," she said, "and you come up here. You and me are going to dig the potatoes."

Robert turned to me, reluctant to leave me alone.

"Don't bother her," Mrs. Spragg said sharply. "She's got her own work to do, and you've got yours." She stepped out of sight from the doorway. "Come along now," she called.

I gave Robert a little push toward the cellar steps. "Do as she says," I whispered. "I'll hurry with the scrubbing, give the windows a lick and a promise, then we'll go home."

Robert went to the garden with Mrs. Spragg. I started

mopping the cellar floor. I fussed and fumed to myself as I swished the wet mop angrily across the stone floor, cutting wide swaths in the dust and dirt. I didn't like the high-handed way Mrs. Spragg had spoken to Robert. He'd only hesitated out of concern for me. She didn't have to speak so cross to him.

As I swiped the mop over the floor for the second time, bringing to light the soft gray color of the stone, I wished I had never laid eyes on Elvira Spragg. Or her dark, dirty cellar. But since I had, I muttered, I would do this job right and give that woman no reason to fault my work.

Instead of the lick and a promise that I had intended to give the windows, they got a first-class cleaning. Not one streak showed on the shining panes of glass.

I put the ladder back where it belonged, wiped the stone tub, and went outside.

Mrs. Spragg called, "Are you finished with the cellar?"

I replied that I was and started toward the garden to help Robert with the potatoes.

"Then get some newspapers off the screened porch," she said. "And lay them by the bins. I'll have to let these potatoes dry before I can store them away."

I changed my course toward the screened porch. The next time someone asks me to do something for them, I won't be so hasty to say yes.

By the time I had the papers spread on the cellar floor, Robert had baskets of potatoes down there, ready to be dumped to dry. When he had emptied the last basket and stacked it with the others, he stood up and gave me a tired smile.

37

"Let's go home," he said, "before she finds something else to be done."

Mrs. Spragg was waiting for us by the outside cellar door. She pressed a coin into Robert's hand, telling him, "Now don't lose that." Then she handed him a pail of tiny potatoes.

Robert thanked her and went on toward the alley.

"This is for you," she said and gave me a dollar bill.

I looked at the money, too surprised to speak. I hadn't expected her to pay us separately. I stammered my thanks and hurried down the alley to where Robert stood waiting for me.

"Seely, look at this big silver dollar," Robert said, his voice filled with awe. "She must mean for us to share it."

"No," I said, "that money is yours. She gave me a dollar too." And I held the bill for him to see.

"Whoo-ee!" he said. "Two bucks and a peck of potatoes to boot! Won't Mom be surprised when she sees this."

I didn't say so to Robert, but I thought that Mom might already know it. She had probably had her talk with Mrs. Spragg about our wages on her way to work this morning. That could account for Mrs. Spragg being so cross earlier. I thought that having Mom drop in at that hour of the day would put anyone's teeth on edge for a while.

Robert put his silver dollar on the kitchen table, and I put my dollar beside it. Then we stood and smiled at each other. At that moment, I didn't think of how much work we had had to do to earn that money, and I'm sure Robert didn't either.

The fire had gone out in the stove, but the water was still warm enough for our baths. We hung a blanket over the line behind the stove and took turns bathing.

"A bath and clean clothes sure makes you feel good," Robert said, dropping onto a chair. "I'm not a bit tired now."

"In that case," I said, "you can help me bring in the washing."

He groaned, but he got up and went with me.

I had watched Mom make starch and dip the clothes before she hung them to dry, but it was plain to see that I hadn't watched her closely enough. When Mom starched a shirt, it dried with just the right firmness to hold its shape. These things were stiff as boards. I couldn't even fold them to fit in the clothes basket.

"Don't break my shirt, Seely," Robert said, and went into a fit of laughing.

"It's not funny," I told Robert. "All that washing and starching was done for nothing." I was ready to cry.

Robert stopped being silly. "Seely, these things can still look all right," he said. "All we have to do is rinse some of the starch out and let them dry again."

It was that simple. And that was what we did.

When Mom got home from work, the house was clean, we were clean, and supper was ready to put on the table. She never once complained of being tired or mentioned how hard she had worked. Robert and I didn't do any complaining either.

I was doing the dishes when Mom asked Robert if we had finished our work for Mrs. Spragg. With a big smile, Robert took the two dollars from his pocket and gave them to Mom.

"We got it all done," he said proudly. "And she gave us that much money and a peck of potatoes for doing it."

Mom smiled and fingered the silver dollar. "That seems more than fair to me, Robert," she said. "I guess I won't have to speak to Elvira about your wages after all."

chapter six

*L*ater that same evening, Gus Tyson backed his truck up to the door of the lean-to shed, shut off the motor, and came into the kitchen.

"Evening, Zel," he greeted Mom. "I had the boys throw the scrap lumber onto the truck, when they cleaned up at the mill today, and I've brought it to you."

Gus seated himself at the kitchen table. Mom poured a cup of coffee and set it before him.

"I'm much obliged to you, Gus," Mom said. "I can use the wood. But with the children's school things to buy, I don't have the money to pay you for the last load of wood you brought me."

Gus Tyson sipped at the hot coffee. "I didn't ask to be paid for the wood," he said. "But I could use help getting it off the truck."

Mom looked at Robert and me, then she jerked her head toward the kitchen door. Robert left the room at once. He needed no further urging. But the long day had caught up with me, and I didn't move quick enough to please Mom. "Seely! Robert can't unload the truck by himself!" She pointed to the door, and I went.

After the lighted kitchen, the shed was pitch black. My foot touched the first step, then reached for the next one. I didn't see Robert sitting there, and I stumbled and fell over him.

I picked myself up and turned toward the dark shape. "For Cripes sake, Robert! Couldn't you have waited for me someplace else?"

"I wasn't waiting for you," he replied angrily. "I'm trying to light this blasted lantern Mrs. Spragg gave me."

He struck a match, and I could see that he was trying to make his two hands do the work of four. "You hold the lantern and keep the globe raised," I said. "I'll hold the match out of the wind and light the wick."

After much juggling of the globe and matches, we got the lantern lit. Robert hung it on a nail in the wall. The light made weird red shadows around the kitchen steps, while the rest of the shed was just faintly lighter than it had been without the lantern.

"I told you this little bugger would come in handy," Robert said.

We climbed onto the truck bed to throw the wood into

the shed. There wasn't enough wood on the truck to keep a fire going long enough to cook a pot of beans.

"Why would Gus Tyson make a special trip to bring in this little dab of wood?" Robert wondered.

"Maybe he had somewhere else to go," I said, "and just dropped this off on his way."

In no time at all we had the wood off the truck and stacked neatly on top of the pile in the shed.

When we went into the house, Gus Tyson asked with feigned surprise, "Have you kids got the truck unloaded already?"

Robert replied that we had.

"Then I guess my visit is over for the night," Gus said, getting to his feet.

Mom walked with him to the door, then locked it behind him. Then she stood there quietly, waiting until the sound of his truck had faded into the night.

"Favors piled on top of more favors," Mom said. "With no hope on earth of ever repaying them." She sighed deeply.

Robert said, "You should've used that silver dollar to pay Gus for the wood."

Mom smiled at him. "Robert, that money is for your books," she said softly.

Then her voice changed, almost as if she was angry about something. "Heaven knows we can use the firewood," Mom said. "But I wish to God he would quit bringing it. I am so far in his debt now that I will die owing favors to Gus Tyson."

After telling Robert and me not to stay up late, Mom went to her bedroom. Robert checked the doors to make sure they were both locked, then we went to bed. I was too tired to write in my diary. But I knew when I got around to it, this day would take up all the spaces on one page.

The light was still on in Mom's room when I went to sleep. It's soft glow made the path from her door to the foot of the stairs. I thought she was probably mulling over the many debts she owed. Especially the ones she said couldn't be paid with all the money in the world.

The door closing behind Mom next morning, as she left for work, woke me. Then I went back to sleep. The next time I woke up, Robert was shaking me and the sun was shining through the loft windows.

"Seely, wake up," Robert said. "Someone is knocking on our door."

I sat up in bed. I was awake, but I wasn't happy about it.

"Then see who it is," I snapped.

Robert started backing down the steps. "I'm not going to open the door," he mumbled. "It's your place to do it. You're the oldest."

"And you're the man of the house!" I shouted after him.

I shucked out of my nightgown, into a dress, and brushed at my hair. As I went down the stairs, I heard the knocking and I yelled, "I'm coming!" I jumped down the last two steps.

"It's probably a Bible salesman," Robert whispered, as he followed me to the door. Mrs. Spragg had told Robert that she had been pestered to death by Bible salesmen lately, and she had warned him to be on the lookout for them.

I jerked open the door, ready to tell whoever waited there that no matter what they were selling we didn't want any. But it was the girl and boy we had seen when we were gathering firewood. They were both smiling, and the girl said, "We didn't aim to wake you. We saw the washing on the line, and we figured you'd been up for hours."

I opened the screen door, and Robert and I stepped outside.

"That's yesterday's wash," I said. "I forgot to bring it in last night."

"She would've thought of it," Robert said, defending me, "but we had other things on our minds."

They both smiled again, showing even white teeth. They were as dark, with black hair, as Robert and I were blond and fair.

"It's nothing to be ashamed of," the girl said. "Why, Dustin and I forgot to tell you we were the Hollis kids. And Mom said to do that, the first thing."

When no one said anything, she added, "I'm Deidre. What's your name?"

I told them our names and asked them to come inside. Mom couldn't have meant anyone like Dustin and Deidre Hollis when she told us not to let strangers into the house.

Deidre shook her head. "We didn't come to visit," she said. "We only stopped to tell you that school starts on Tuesday, and we'll be here to walk with you."

"We live with Grandpa Hollis on Bottom Road,"

45

Dustin added, and motioned toward the end of the alley. "Dad left us when the stone mill closed down, and we've been with Grandpa ever since."

"Mom doesn't like it," Deidre said. "But she says that's where Duncan Hollis left her. And that's where he'll find her, if he ever comes back."

Dustin said, "Where's your folks? I don't see them around. Did your old man run out on you, too?"

Robert stepped back as if Dustin had swung a fist at him.

"Our dad died last winter," I said. "And Mom went to work to support us. That's why she isn't home with Robert and me."

"Anytime that you and Robert want to, you can come to our house," Dustin said. "Mom is always home."

He touched Deidre's arm, and they turned and went off across the yard.

"Come back again," I called after them.

Deidre just waved her hand, and she didn't answer.

Robert and I went inside, latching the screen door behind us and leaving the main door open.

"It will sure be good to have someone to walk into school with me on Tuesday," I said. Even after being the new one in class as many times as I had, I still dreaded that first day of school.

"It don't seem fair," Robert said. "I'm the one who really needs somebody to go to school with me, and you get two of them."

I set up the ironing board to press our school clothes, then I went to bring the things in from the line. Robert went with me, talking faster than I could count.

"This has been some week," he said, rolling the damp overalls into a tight ball. "We've worked and made money, and we've got two new friends."

"Let's hope the friends will outlast the money," I said.

Robert kind of smiled and picked up one side of the basket to help carry it inside. At the kitchen door, he set the basket down and went back for the clothespins.

I wasn't used to an electric iron yet. I kept forgetting that it didn't cool off like a flat iron, and I scorched things. But today, everything came out smooth and crisp, with not one sign of a scorch. Even Robert's overalls turned out like new.

Later that afternoon, Robert and I sat on the back steps and cleaned and polished our shoes. I wondered aloud how long these shoes were going to last us.

"As long as they have to," Robert said. "And then awhile."

I knew what he meant. When the seams split, or the soles fell off these shoes, we would wear them that way. Dad wasn't here to sew up the seams and put on new half-soles, so we could get another month's wear out of them.

As it sometimes happened, now that Robert and I were together all the time, he seemed to be following my train of thought with his own. Or maybe it was because we were handling the shoes that Dad came to mind.

"Seely, do you ever miss Dad?"

"All the time," I replied.

I stood up to take my shoes inside.

"Then why don't you ever want to talk about him?"

"Robert, talking about Dad won't make it any easier to get along without him." I touched his arm and gave him a small pat. "Come on inside," I said. "Mom will be home soon."

I went into the house and left Robert sitting on the steps, staring into space and absently drawing the shine cloth back and forth across the scuffed toe of his shoe.

chapter seven

Tuesday morning, the first day of school, Robert and I were scrubbed and brushed and dressed in our best, waiting for the Hollises. The yellow dress I had on had lost most of its original color except under the collar and cuffs and along the seams. The dress wasn't linen, but it wrinkled like linen. Every time I sat down the skirt rumpled like a washboard.

Robert had grown taller over the summer, or else the overalls had shrunk in the wash. I let the gallusses out as far as they would go, but the overalls barely reached his shoetops.

"It's the starch in them," I told Robert. "They'd hang longer on you if they weren't so stiff."

"I'll bet they wouldn't scratch as bad either," he said, tugging at the seat of his pants.

We took turns watching for Deidre and Dustin Hollis. It was getting late and there was no sign of them. I wondered whether we shouldn't go ahead without them. This could be their idea of a good joke, I told Robert, making us wait until we would be late for the first day of school.

We didn't really know them. They could be the kind who would hold us up to ridicule, once they were with their friends at school. I started to tell Robert we wouldn't wait any longer, when he called, "Seely, they're here," and ran to meet them.

I should not have wasted a minute wondering about the Hollis kids. Dustin had on a pair of overalls that made Robert's overalls look good, and the red cotton dress that Deidre was wearing looked as worn and faded as my yellow one.

If I had been using my head, I would've known that the Hollises were no better off that we were. "Water seeks its own level," Mom was fond of saying. Had they been well to do, Deidre and Dustin would not have sought us out in the first place.

I found out that Deidre was eighteen and a year ahead of me in school.

"We can sit next to each other in the assembly hall," Deidre said. "I'll take a desk in the first row of seniors, and you can pick a desk in the last row of juniors, then we'll be side by side. I don't know about the schools you've gone to before, but here we keep all our books in our desks in the assembly hall."

I was pleased that Deidre wanted to sit near me. I couldn't do much better than having a senior for a friend, I thought.

When I asked her where I could get used books for my classes, Deidre said, "You can have the books I used last year. The books haven't changed since the Depression started, nor the subjects either."

I offered to pay her for the books, but she said they hadn't cost her anything.

"When Fay Simpson was a junior," Deidre said, "I was one grade behind her, but I did all her lessons for her. Then when school was out, Fay gave me her books."

She hooked her arm through mine, and smiled. "Fay graduated last year with my help, and I inherited her senior books."

I was amazed. "You must be awfully bright," I said.

Deidre shook her dark curls. "Not really," she said. "A body doesn't have to be smart to help a Simpson. They're all as dumb as dirt."

Later, when I had to sit next to Arvella Simpson in homeroom, I understood what Deidre meant about the Simpsons.

To my surprise, Robert and Dustin turned down the walk toward the grade school. I watched as they both passed through the wide doors and went into the schoolhouse.

"I'm glad Dustin is taking Robert to school," I said. "He's been dreading to go in there by himself."

"Dustin goes to the elementary school," Deidre said.

"He missed a good deal of school when he was younger," she explained, "because he was sick a lot, and he had to make it up. He's in the eighth grade this year."

I felt like I ought to say something. But nothing that came to my mind seemed to be the right thing. Finally, I said, "Robert will be pleased. He was wishing for someone to go to school with him this year."

Deidre smiled and began to tell me about the high school and what I could expect there this morning. "It never changes," she said.

The school was just as Deidre had said it would be. As we entered the building, we were given a registration form and directed to our section of the assembly hall. Deidre gave me a list of the third year books that she had at home, so I would know what classes to sign up for. By the time I had filled in the blanks on the registration papers, the first and second year classes had already been moved from the assembly hall, and it was the third year's turn to go to their homeroom.

Everything and everyone moved swiftly and smoothly. It seemed like no time at all before the dismissal bell rang. The first day of school was only a half day. We all streamed out of the building. As far as being the new girl in school went, I was only one among many. A lot of them seemed to be strangers.

"How did it go this morning?" Deidre asked, when I met her coming out of school. "Could you use the books I have for you?"

"Things went fine," I replied. "And I can use all the books."

Robert and Dustin Hollis were waiting for us on the

low stone wall in front of the schoolhouse. When he saw me, Robert jumped down and came running to meet me.

"Dustin knows a shortcut to his house," Robert said. "Could we walk home with him?"

"Not so fast, Robert," I said. "Where's your list for books and supplies that you'll need?"

"Right here," he said, slapping his hip pocket. "Where is your list?"

Deidre said, "Seely is getting her books from me. She doesn't need one."

She slipped her arm through mine, and we moved away from the school. "Why don't you walk home with Dustin and me?" she asked. "You could pick up your books and take them home with you this afternoon."

Robert was teasing to go home with Dustin. And I thought it would be good to have the books on hand to show Mom when she got home tonight. But I had my doubts about going to the Hollis house so soon after meeting Dustin and Deidre.

Reluctantly, I said all right. "You walked the long way round to come to school with us," I told Deidre. "It is only fair that we take the shortcut home with you."

Not far from the high school, the paved street gave way to crushed stone, and the houses got farther apart. When the graveled road changed to a plain old dirt track through the trees, there wasn't a house to be seen anywhere.

Dustin pointed to a narrow trail that branched off through the trees. "We're nearly home," he said. "We live right at the bottom of that hill."

The narrow track that we followed downhill looked as though the earth had been scraped away, leaving only hard rock and shale underfoot. But the path was strewn with fallen leaves, making it easy to stumble over a hidden stone.

Deidre walked close beside me, cautioning me to watch my step and pointing out any snag.

"I'm used to the hills and hollows and country roads," I told her. "It's the city streets that I don't understand."

"We've brought you the way we always take when we go to town," Dustin said. "It's an uphill climb as we're going, but when we're coming home with our arms loaded, it's downhill all the way."

At the foot of the hill, Bottom Road ran between the woods and the river beyond the clearing. The big farmhouse where Deidre and Dustin lived sat about halfway between the hill and the road. A gray ribbon of smoke rose from its chimney, signaling the preparation of the noon meal. As we crossed the backyard to the house, I could smell fresh-baked yeast bread.

"Maybe we shouldn't go in," I said. "Your mother will have dinner ready, and we'd just be in the way."

"No, you wouldn't," Deidre replied. "Mom will be right glad to see you. She doesn't get much company out here."

chapter eight

When Robert and I followed Dustin and Deidre into the house, neither Mrs. Hollis nor the old man took any notice of us. Mrs. Hollis was standing at the cookstove, stirring a pot with one hand and wiping sweat from her face with the other, never once taking her eyes off the giant-sized old man standing near her.

I knew he had to be Grandpa Hollis. And I thought he looked like a man who would take some watching. He had a great mane of white hair that touched his shoulders, a big nose, and a full mustache and long white beard that covered the bib of his worn overalls. He leaned his weight on a knobby cane and glared at Mrs. Hollis. She glared back at him.

I stopped just inside the kitchen door. It was obvious we had walked into the middle of a family quarrel, and I hoped our presence would bring a lull in the battle.

Dustin didn't seem to notice anything out of the ordinary. He took Robert by the hand and went straight as a homing pigeon to the side of the fierce-looking old man.

"Grandpa, this is my friend Robert," Dustin said, sharing his smile equally between Robert and his grandfather. "Robert is going to run the traps with me this winter," he added.

Grandpa Hollis seemed to take no notice of Robert. But his free hand found Robert's head and rested lightly, his fingers gently smoothing the fine honey-colored hair beneath his hand.

"Mersy Hollis," Grandpa shouted across the room, "are you aiming to feed this hungry pack of young'uns, or do you figure to forego dinner to spit fire at me?"

Deidre's mother flashed the old man a look that would have singed the hair off a plucked chicken. Then she turned to stir the pot that was simmering on the stove.

"Deidre, put the plates on the table," Mrs. Hollis said quietly.

Deidre moved quickly to place six plates around the table.

"We only stopped to get some books for school," I said. "We can't stay to eat."

Mersy Hollis lifted the kettle from the stove and set it in the middle of the table. Then she looked at me and smiled.

56

"We expected you to stay for dinner," she said. "The kids said they would bring you home with them, so I made plenty for us all."

She brought two loaves of bread to the table and sliced each loaf into thick chunks.

"Everybody sit down," she said. "Dinner is ready."

We sat quietly at the table while Mersy Hollis put a chunk of bread on each plate, covered it with meat and gravy from the kettle, and then she passed the plates to us. Grandpa Hollis and the boys were served first, but no one took a bite until Mrs. Hollis picked up her knife and fork.

Everyone ate for some time without saying a word. Then Grandpa Hollis said, "Daughter, that's the best bread and squirrel gravy that I've had in a long time."

"Thank you, Dun," Mersy Hollis replied quietly.

I guess they had been waiting for old Dun Hollis to comment on the dinner. Afterwards everyone began to talk.

When the plates were wiped clean of gravy, with the last piece of bread, Dustin turned to his grandpa. "Tell Robert about the beaver sign you saw down along White River."

"You boys have got no business that far downriver," the old man said. "If you want to trap, set them this side of the river bridge. And don't cross over White River. There's plenty of good trapping spots between the bridge and our boundary line," he added.

"But a good beaver pelt would bring more at Mike Grecco's store," Dustin argued, "than a half dozen raccoon and muskrat hides."

Grandpa Hollis cleared his throat loudly and fingered

his beard and mustache with a thumb and forefinger. "No use talking about it, son," he said. "Time enough for talking when the traps are ready to use."

He turned to Robert. "Did you ever do any trapping, boy?"

Robert shook his head. "No sir."

"Then you've got a heap to learn before the first freeze," the old man told him.

When the table was cleared, I started to help Deidre with the dishes, and Robert went to the barn with Dustin and Grandpa Hollis to look at steel traps.

Mersy Hollis asked me where we went to church, and when I told her we hadn't found one yet, she invited us to go to church with them on Sunday.

"Mom would like that," I said. "But she will probably have to work on Sunday."

"Come if you can," she said. "We don't leave the house till after nine."

As soon as the dishes were dried and put away, I called Robert to the house. Deidre brought the books to me in a flour sack. I slung it over my shoulder, and we left for home. We still had all our chores to do and supper to fix, before Mom got home.

Bottom Road seemed all uphill from the Hollis farm. There were wide open fields on either side of the road, and high wooded hills beyond the clearings. This country didn't look a lot different from Greene County, I thought.

"All that ground belongs to Dustin's grandpa," Robert said. "And the river belongs to Grandpa Hollis too. All the way to the Bottom Road bridge over White River."

I commented that I didn't know a person could own a river. I thought it ran free like the wind and wild animals.

Robert was nodding his head vigorously. "Grandpa Hollis owns it all," he said. "He owns the wild animals that live in the woods and along his share of the river. That's why Dustin and I are allowed to set traps there this winter."

As hot as it was on this open uphill road, winter seemed a long way off to me. Too far away to be making any positive plans for it. Yet I knew these warm days couldn't last. Already we had heard the wild geese flying south. Any night now we'd have a killing frost, and then winter would be a matter of days away.

"Hey," Robert said, when we came to the alley a few minutes later, "the Hollises don't live far away at all."

Later, when we were doing our chores, he said, "Seely, the Hollises are good people, aren't they?"

I said that I thought so. And that's what I told Mom that evening, when I was showing her the books Deidre had given me.

"You don't need to worry about buying books for me," I said. "Deidre Hollis gave me hers."

"Seely, I'd rather pay the girl," Mom said, "and not have you beholden to her. Besides, she might get a chance to sell them later on, and she'd want them back."

"She's not like that, Mom," I said. "The Hollises are good people."

"I'd have to see that for myself," Mom replied.

"Then why don't you go see them?" I said. "Mrs. Hollis invited us to go to church with her on Sunday.

She said she'd be looking for us about nine, should you care to go."

"There is no use to talk about it," Mom said. "You know I have to work on Sunday."

She picked up the list of Robert's books and supplies and started for her room. "I'll be late getting home from work tomorrow," she said. "I'll be going to the store to get what I can of these things."

It was dark when Mom got home the next day, but she had bought all the books Robert needed, paper and pencils for us both, and she said she still had money left over. The books were old and marked with many names on the flyleaf, but they would last another year.

When I asked Mom how on earth she had got so much for so little, she said, "Nedra Noyer took me to the Salvation Army Store. They have everything there that a body could possibly want. I picked up a pair of work shoes while I was there," she added. "They cost me fifty cents, and they are hardly broken in yet."

I had heard of the Salvation Army, but I didn't know they had a store where people could buy used things. I figured it must be a lot like the poor box at church, where really poor people picked around for clothes that would fit them. Only at the Salvation Army Store you had to pay for the stuff you got.

After Mom went to bed, I told Robert not to say a word about where he got his books. "Should anyone ask you," I said, "just say, 'Where do you generally get used books?' and let it go at that."

"What's wrong with saying Salvation Army Store?"

"I don't know," I said, "so don't do it."

Dustin and Deidre came by the next morning to walk to school with us. Then, in the afternoon, Robert went home with Dustin by the shortcut, and Deidre walked home with me. And so it went for the rest of the week. One afternoon, I helped Mrs. Spragg clean her kitchen. On Friday, Robert dug the onions in her garden and carried them to the cellar. Mrs. Spragg gave us each fifty cents for our work, and we gave the money to Mom.

Saturday morning when I got up, I found a note from Mom on the kitchen table telling me to change the beds and do the washing. Robert was to make a quart of furniture polish and clean everything.

"Just put two tablespoons of olive oil and two of vinegar in a quart of warm water," she wrote. "And be sure to rub the furniture till it's dry."

Robert helped me get the water on to heat for the washing, and while the water was getting hot, he washed the dust and dirt off everything in the house, and I polished it all dry. We even cleaned the old turquoise pie safe and kitchen cabinet while we were at it.

Later that afternoon, Dustin Hollis came to see Robert. I was taking the washing off the line, and Robert was tossing the clothespins at the basket, for want of something better to do. His chores were done.

"Robert, we're going to smoke the steel traps," Dustin said. "And Grandpa thought you ought to see how it's done."

Robert dropped the handful of wooden pins and looked at me. I finished folding the sheet in my hands and put it in the basket. Mom wouldn't like it. But if he was back here when she got home, Mom wouldn't say too much. Or so I reasoned.

"Robert, you go ahead with Dustin," I said. "If you are going to be a trapper, you should know all you can about it. But you be home here before dark," I added.

Robert smiled and nodded his head, then he struck off across the yard toward the alley. He stopped and looked back when he realized that Dustin wasn't right behind him.

Dustin said, "Seely, it might be after dark before we get the traps done. It takes a while for the wood to burn down to the ashes. But I'll bring him home," he said earnestly, "when we are finished with the traps."

"You mean to burn the traps in the fire and then leave them in the ashes?"

"That's to get the scent of people and other animals off the traps," Dustin said. Then his voice took on a teasing note as he said, "Seely, are you sure you wouldn't like to run a trapline with me?"

I said, "Heaven forbid!" and went to take the rest of the wash off the line.

When I returned to the basket with an armload of laundry, the boys were nearly at the end of the alley. I took the wash inside and ironed until it was time to start supper.

Supper time came and went. Neither Mom nor Robert showed up to eat with me. I put the cornbread in the warming oven, so it wouldn't dry out, pushed the potato soup and coffee to the back of the stove to keep warm, then I sat down to wait for whomever came first. And I thought, if the old saying was true—that God looked after fools and babies—then He had better see to it that Robert got home before Mom did.

chapter nine

Robert and Dustin had been at the house long enough to eat a bowl of potato soup and get a checker game going before Mom got home that night. I heard her coming slowly up the cinder path, and I went to open the door for her. Mom still insisted that we keep the door locked at all times.

"I've kept supper warm for you," I said as soon as Mom came in, hoping to forestall any unpleasantness she might come up with when she found Dustin here with Robert and me.

Mom was surprised to see Dustin, but not displeased. "I had a bite of supper at the hotel," she said.

She sat down at the table where Robert and Dustin

had their heads bent over the checkerboard. Mom watched as Dustin moved one of the red disks. Robert picked up his one crowned piece and jumped all the red disks, clearing the board of all Dustin's checkers. Robert laughed and Dustin groaned and dropped his head to the table.

"You must be Robert's friend, Dustin," Mom said with a smile.

Dustin raised his head and smiled back at her. "You couldn't tell it by the way he whopped me at checkers," he said.

He got to his feet and moved away from the table. "I've got to get home," he said. "Mom will think the bogey-man has me, for sure."

Mom nodded her head, the smile still in her eyes. "Dustin, tell your mother I would be real pleased to walk to church with her in the morning. And much obliged for the chance," she added.

Dustin's smile lit up his whole face. "I sure will," he said. "Mom will be right glad to hear it."

His feet leaped the back steps, and he hit the ground running. A moment later we heard a whoop, like the sound of a wild Indian.

"I'll bet Dustin is afraid of the dark," Robert said.

"No," Mom said, "he's just young and full of vinegar."

I poured a cup of coffee and set it in front of Mom. "How did you manage to get out of working to-morrow?" I asked her.

"By doing two day's work in one day's time," Mom replied. "And there were times today when I had my doubts that I could do it," she added.

"I know what you mean," I said. "That's how I felt

when I finished the ironing and knew I still had supper to fix."

Mom asked if we had done everything she had on the list for us to do. I said we had and some things she hadn't listed. "That's good," she said.

Mom finished her coffee, then she went to her room. Robert and I neatened up the kitchen and we went to bed. But before I blew out the light, I opened my diary to September 1937 and filled one whole page with what the day had been like.

Mersy Hollis and Deidre and Dustin were ready and waiting for us when we got to the Hollis farm. Mersy asked us into the house so Mom could say hello to Grandpa Hollis.

"Don't you want to go to church with us?" Mom asked him as we were leaving.

"You ladies take the young'uns on to church," Dun Hollis replied. "That Loon Creek Christian Church is the last place on earth I want to go to."

"Dun, when the time comes," Mersy said, "I'll see that it is."

Dun Hollis snorted and turned away. Mersy smiled to herself.

"Grandpa Hollis claims to own the Loon Creek Church," Deidre said, "but he hasn't once set foot in the place."

"Deidre," Mersy Hollis scolded, "don't speak disrespectful of your grandpa. He has every right to say what he does about the church."

As we walked down the road toward the church,

Mersy Hollis explained why old Dun Hollis felt that he had some claim on it. "The members of the Loon Creek Christian Church tried for years to buy that piece of ground where the church sits," Mersy Hollis said. "But Dun didn't want to part with it. They finally gave up on that spot and built their church up the hollow between White River and Loon Creek. Then when the floods came last January," Mersy went on, "the flood waters washed the church downriver and left it sitting on Dun's property. Old Dun said it looked to him like the Lord had chosen that piece of ground for His house. So he gave it to the church."

"That seems right generous of Mr. Hollis," Mom said.

Mersy nodded her head. "The Lord never made a more generous man than Dun Hollis," she said. "Nor a more contrarier one," she added under her breath.

Deidre and I followed Mom and Mersey Hollis into the church. But when we saw Robert and Dustin had stopped at a pew near the door, we dropped back and slid onto the seat next to them.

I kept my face turned attentively toward the pulpit, but when the sermon was over I couldn't recall a word the preacher had spoken. And I doubt that anyone else could either. It was like Nellie Fender used to say about the Reverend Mr. Paully; the preacher could see that the folks had come to church for peace and quiet, and he didn't want to disturb them.

When we got back to the Hollis place, Robert teased to stay with Dustin and come home later. But Mom said he was needed at home.

"You know better than to pester to stay at this time

67

of day," Mom told Robert, as we walked on toward home. "Them folks are getting ready to eat their dinner, and they would feel obliged to ask you to the table."

"I didn't think of that," Robert said.

He could understand Mom's reasoning though. In these times, folks fixed just enough food to go once around the table, unless they knew beforehand there would be extra mouths to feed. Any unexpected guests at mealtime meant watery soup or thin gravy and smaller portions for the family.

The day was warm, and Mom seemed in no hurry to get home. We walked slowly, stopping often to rest and admire the color of the trees across the way.

Mom said that she was glad we had found good neighbors to go to church with. "Especially this close to home," she added.

I figured it must be a mile or more from our house to the Loon Creek Church. But I didn't say anything. A mile didn't seem very far on a day like this one.

Fanny Phillips and Gus Tyson were sitting on our back steps when we got home.

Mom said, "Why didn't you go on in? The door is open."

Mom insisted that we keep the doors locked while we were in the house, yet she never locked a door behind her when we were going away for a while.

"We just got here," Fanny replied. She got to her feet and followed Mom into the house.

Gus and Fanny had dinner with us. Then afterwards, Fanny gave Robert a haircut. When she was finished with

Robert, Fanny said, "Zel, why don't you sit down here and let me bob your hair?"

Before Mom could answer her, Gus Tyson said, "Fanny, you keep your clippers off Zel's hair. It looks fine the way she wears it now."

Mom's face got pink. She put both hands to her hair and smoothed the loose tendrils back into the bun, "Maybe I will," she said, "one of these days."

She seemed not to notice the look that Gus Tyson gave his sister. But I'd be willing to bet that after Gus got through talking to Fanny, she would never again suggest cutting Mom's hair.

I had to go help Elvira Spragg do some cooking and baking in preparation for a visit from her nephew and his family. When I got home, Gus and Fanny had gone back to Jubilee.

I gave Mom the fifty cents that Mrs. Spragg had paid me, and she put it with my other earnings.

"You'll soon have enough money saved to get yourself a warm winter coat," Mom said, shaking the tea tin where she stashed my earnings.

"Some of that money belongs to Robert," I said. "It wouldn't be fair for him to do my chores, when I work, and not get something for it."

"By the time you need a coat," Mom said, "there will be enough here to get you both one."

She took the tea tin to her room, and I went to the stove to see what we were having for supper.

I took a hot biscuit from the pan just as Mom came into the kitchen. She frowned at me. "We'll eat supper as soon as Robert gets here," she said. "Dustin came for him right after you went to the Spragg house. He should be home any minute."

"I'll just wander down Bottom Road a piece," I said, "and see if I can hurry him along."

"You do that," Mom said. "And don't dilly-dally on the way. It will be dark soon."

Once on Bottom Road, where I knew no one could see me, I started running. I ran for a while, then I slowed to a lope. When the Hollis farmhouse came in sight, I was just walking fast.

As I was crossing the yard, I met Mersy Hollis coming from the barn. "You looking for Deidre, she's in the barn with the boys," she said. I thanked her and turned down the path to the barn.

Robert and Dustin were picking the steel traps out of the ashes, then shaking them vigorously to get rid of the dust. Holding the traps gingerly by the ring at the end of the chain, they passed them to Deidre to hang on nails along the crossbeams of the barn.

"I was getting ready to leave," Robert said quickly, when he saw me at the door.

"We only have a few more traps to shake," Dustin said. "Then we'll be done."

I looked at Deidre. "They've promised me the first beaver skin for helping them." She laughed.

Dustin finished shaking an ash-covered trap and held it out to me. I took it from his hand, careful to touch only the ring, and hung it on a nail.

"Now I get the second beaver you catch," I said.

"Only if you skin it yourself," Dustin replied.

70

Deidre and I hung the rest of the traps. Then we left the barn so the boys could strip off their clothes and shake the dust and ashes from them.

"Mom and Grandpa have been at each other's throats ever since we got home from church this morning," Deidre said, "but they won't carry on the fight in front of strangers."

This was only my second visit to the Hollis house, but I guess that was enough times for me to lose my standing as a stranger or company. Mersy and Grandpa Hollis went right on arguing as if I wasn't there.

I was glad when Dustin and Robert came to the house, and Robert and I could go home. I liked Mersy Hollis, and I liked the grandfather. But I didn't want to be around them when they were angry with each other.

chapter ten

*T*he small chair that I got from Mrs. Spragg's junk pile fit perfectly in the space beneath the south window in my loft room. Mom didn't seem to notice I'd brought it in. I could sit there in the morning, before it was time to leave for school, and look out the window, watching as the late fall haze rose and hovered over the far hills in shades of pearl and lavender. I knew that by midmorning the haze would be scattered like smoke. Gone like the daydreams I fashioned as I walked to school and back each day. But the sight of the haze-covered hills, like the dreams, helped me to get through the day.

At night, when supper was over and the chores were

done, I would sit on the chair by the window and write in my diary. On the very worst days, I would use the blank sides of the pages of my workbooks and write down the things that happened at school during the day, pretending they had happened to someone else. Writing it down as a story seemed to help me forget the slighting remarks of some of the others in my classes and make it easier for me to get out of bed the next day and start all over again.

Scrubbing and cleaning the Spragg house, and the other houses where Elvira Spragg had gotten work for me, had made my hands break out in a rash and burn something fierce. Mom said it was the strong soap I had to use. Whatever it was, my hands cracked and itched. When I forgot and scratched them, my hands would bleed.

The kids in my class at school made a big show of not touching anything that I'd had my hands on first. When work sheets were taken up in class, my papers were picked up by one corner and carried to the teacher's desk. Arvella Simpson told anyone who would listen that I had the Seven Year Itch.

I told Mom that the kids at school thought that I had the itch. They wouldn't have a thing to do with me. I begged to quit school until my hands were healed, but she wouldn't hear of it.

"Pay them no mind, Seely," Mom said. "We know it's not the itch. And that's all that matters."

But it mattered to me. I spent each day wishing it was over, and living for Saturday and Sunday when there was no school.

Fanny Phillips sent a jar of mutton tallow salve by Gus

Tyson when he brought firewood, and it seemed to help my hands. But about the time the cracks and rawness started to heal, I would get word that someone wanted their house cleaned. When I was done with the scrubbing, the rash and rawness would be back on my hands.

Deidre Hollis said that I should refuse to do housework. "Your hands will never heal, as long as you do it," she said.

Even though Deidre was my friend, I couldn't tell her that I had to work. We needed every cent I could make. It would soon be too cold to wear a sweater to school, and Robert had outgrown his coat from last year. Mom seemed to think we'd have the money for new coats, but I doubted it. It would take more dimes and nickels than I'd made so far to pay for even one coat.

The soapy water, when I did the week's laundry, stung my hands like hot coals. In the summer we could do the washing any day we chose to, but during the school year it had to be done on Saturday. We needed the clean clothes for the next week.

I was glad when Dustin came to see Robert. It was still early in the day, but Robert had his chores done. He had filled the woodbox, made his bed, and he'd been making a nuisance of himself ever since. He didn't want to do the things I asked him to do. He wanted to scrub the clothes on the washboard, and he didn't know how.

"Today we're setting the traplines," Dustin said. "Grandpa sent me to tell you, then I have to get back home. He'll need help making the stakes for the traps."

For the past week Robert and Dustin had tracked through the woods and down White River searching for

74

likely spots to set their traps. They had even talked Deidre and me into saving table scraps and tinfoil wrapper to use as bait for the traps.

"Deidre will help me carry the traps to the boundary line," Dustin told Robert. "You can meet us there."

"Is Deidre going to set traps with you?" I asked.

Dustin grinned. "Yeah," he said. "She's still trying to earn that first beaver pelt."

"Then I'll be with Robert to meet you at the boundary," I said.

Dustin said they'd see us later and took off, running toward Bottom Road and home.

Now that Robert and I had something to look forward to when the washing was done, he didn't mind helping me. We whipped through it like it was a game we were playing.

We crossed Bottom Road and climbed the fence on the other side, hurrying to cross the open field and gain the shelter of the woods before anyone saw us. Robert said he didn't know who owned this field, but until we were over Grandpa Hollis's line fence, we were trespassing.

"It's not far, once we get to the trees," Robert said. "We go up the hill, and the boundary line runs along the top of it."

It sounded easy, but there was no worn trail up the hill. We had to pick our way through thickets and berry patches to get to the tall timber. Where the underbrush had thinned out, we could see straight up to the top of the hill, and the sun lighting the bare crest.

On the ridge of the hill, where Dustin and Deidre were

waiting for us, we could see for miles. Down in the White River bottom land, acres and acres of brown-leafed corn was waiting to be harvested. Beyond the river, where we were forbidden to go, tree-covered hills rose and rolled toward higher hills, the bare-limbed trees stretching far into the distance.

Dustin suggested we split up in two groups. "We'll meet at the river bridge," he said, "when we're done setting the traps."

We all agreed that was a good idea.

"I'll take the river," Robert said. "Who wants to go with me?"

Deidre picked up one of the gunny sacks that held the steel traps and started down the hill toward the river. Robert followed her with the holding stakes and the bait bucket.

Dustin and I took the hills above the cornfield, following the markers that he and Robert had left there earlier in the week.

When we got to a marker, I drove the stake through the ring at the end of the chain, securing the trap. Dustin spread the wicked-looking jaws and baited the tongue with tinfoil.

"I wish that farmer would shuck his corn and get it out of the bottom," Dustin said. "How can we tempt a raccoon with a shiny piece of paper, when it's got a whole cornfield to choose from?"

"Isn't that your grandpa's cornfield?"

"It's his ground," Dustin replied. "But the corn belongs to the man who rents it from Grandpa. That's where we get the money to live," he explained.

76

It was late in the afternoon when Dustin and I staked and set our last trap and headed downhill toward the river bridge. Dustin had bits of leaves and black woods dirt stuck to him from head to toe. And I knew that I looked as bad as he did, if not worse.

Dustin smiled at me and said, "Seely, you make one fine trapper."

I slid on the dead leaves, and he offered his hand for support. I smiled at Dustin and placed my raw red hand in his. His fingers closed gently around my hand, and we walked that way to the river.

Robert and Deidre were waiting at the bridge when we got there. I thought of the work still waiting at home, and I wished aloud that I knew a shorter way to our alley.

"There's no shorter way than straight up Bottom Road," Dustin said, setting out at such a fast pace the rest of us found it hard to keep up with him.

Before we left the Hollises, the boys settled on a route for running the traplines. Dustin would take the hill traps, meeting Robert where we had met today, then the two of them would check downriver together. That way, Robert wouldn't have to deal with the trapped animals alone, Dustin said. "Not till you get the hang of it."

With a "See you in church," Robert and I waved to Dustin and Deidre and went on up the road.

When we got home, Robert built a fire in the cookstove and put a tub of water on to heat for our bath. I took the washing off the line, folded the things to be put away, and sprinkled the ones that had to be ironed later.

I was glad that Mom took supper at the hotel on the

77

night when she worked late. I didn't have to make supper at any given time. Robert and I could eat whenever we got hungry.

After Robert and I had our bath and I'd finished the ironing, I smeared mutton tallow salve on my hands. Fanny Phillips sent more salve every time Gus Tyson delivered the wood. She swore that mutton tallow would heal anything. Even my hands. It should, I thought. Anything that smelled as bad as that salve ought to be good for something.

Mom came home while I was salving my hands. She sniffed and fanned the air in front of her face. "Land's sake, Seely," she said. "Couldn't you wait and put that stuff on your hands when you go to bed? You're stinking up the whole house."

"Then I'll take my stinking hands and go to bed!"

I grabbed the jar of salve off the table and headed for the steps to the loft.

"Seely," Mom said in a tired voice.

I acted like I didn't hear her. I went up the steps to my room and sat by the window in the dark, rubbing the foul-smelling ointment into my hands.

She hadn't asked how my hands felt after scrubbing on the washboard, I thought. She could only complain of the odor when I tried to soothe the soreness. It had been at her insistence that I used this homemade remedy. I wouldn't have touched it, if she hadn't kept harping at me to try it.

The light from the kitchen made the loft room gray and shadowy. I didn't need to light the lamp to get undressed and into my nightgown.

The mutton tallow salve had soaked into my hands. They were not sticky, but the smell was still there.

Mom must have heard me moving around upstairs because she called, "Seely, come down here."

I moved to the edge of the balcony and looked down. I could just see Mom sitting at the kitchen table and she was alone. Robert had gone to bed.

"I'm ready for bed," I answered. And because her words to me earlier still rankled, I added, "And my hands still stink."

She turned toward the sound of my voice. "Come here, Seely," Mom said firmly. "I won't tell you again."

I went downstairs and sat at the table as she told me to do.

"Seely," Mom said, then hesitated as if she didn't quite know how to start. "There is no room in this family for hurt feelings. We can't afford to feel sorry for ourselves and get on edge at every word."

She paused, and I thought she'd had her say. But she hadn't.

"And I want you to know right now," she added, "I won't tolerate temper fits from either one of you. Especially not from a girl your age."

When I didn't say anything, Mom kind of cleared her throat and said quietly, "I aimed to tell you to let the washing go and save your hands. But I forgot it."

She put her hands to her face, then slowly pushed her hair back.

"The washing wasn't so bad," I said. "Robert helped me."

"I ask too much of you and Robert," Mom said.

"There is never time for any enjoyment. But this is the only way I know to survive here." She added, "I can't do it alone."

Mom had been on her feet since four o'clock this morning, and it was now past ten at night. But she hadn't said one word about the hours she had worked, or the many tubs of dough and trays of rolls she'd had to lift from oven to rack, to get her pay. She had spoken only of the hardship she felt Robert and I were going through.

I felt my face grow hot with shame for the way I had acted earlier.

"Are we going to church tomorrow?" I raised my eyes to Mom's face for her answer.

There was just a hint of a smile showing in her eyes, as Mom said, "We are. If I can get out of bed."

She pushed back her chair. "I'll leave the light burning till you get to the loft."

I scrambled up the steps. Mom turned out the light. But before I went to bed I gave my hands another dosing of salve and pulled a pair of old socks over them to keep the stinking stuff off my bed.

chapter eleven

We awoke on Sunday morning to a gray and overcast sky. Just overnight, the south wind and sunny skies of yesterday had changed to a cold northeast wind that seemed to go right through to the bone. Mom said it looked to be blowing up an early snow.

"Squaw Winter, the Indians used to call it," she said. "When this passes we can expect a warm spell. Indian Summer. Then the winter really sets in for good," she added.

"Why do people always say that winter sets in for good?" I said. "I can't see anything good about it."

Mom just looked at me and went on getting the stewing chicken ready to put in the pot. The chicken would boil and simmer on the stove while we were at church. Then when we got home, it would be nearly ready for the dumplings.

Instead of wearing her warm coat to church, Mom wore a sweater, the same as Robert and me. She didn't mention being cold, but long before we got to the Hollises', Mom had folded her arms across her chest, and she was hugging herself to keep warm.

Mersy and Deidre Hollis had on coats, but Dustin was wearing the same sweater he wore to school every day.

"We had such a warm pretty day yesterday," Mom told Mersy, "that I didn't expect to need a heavy coat this morning."

Mersy Hollis smiled. "More than likely, we'll be carrying our coats on the way home," she said.

But when we came out of the church, the wind was whipping a fine spray of snow across the country that stung our faces like bits of broken glass. We ducked our heads against the wind and hurried up Bottom Road.

At the Hollises, Mersy asked us in to get warm. But Mom said there was no telling about this weather. It could get worse by the minute. "We'd best not stop," she said, "but get on home."

Head down against the wind, we kept on going. The sloping hill up Bottom Road from the Hollises was the longest, coldest hill I'd ever climbed. When we walked into the house, Mom rubbed her arms and shivered. "I can't remember when I've been so glad to get in out of the weather," she said. I felt the same way.

Without being told to do it, Robert built up the fire

in the cookstove, filled the woodbox in the kitchen and front room, and laid a fire in the big air-tight Florence heating stove; ready to be lit at a moment's notice.

I turned on the water to fill the reservoir on the cookstove, and suddenly I had to go so bad that I thought I would never make it to the privy. I hurried there and back. As I came through the shed to the kitchen door, I noticed for the first time how low we were on firewood. Less than a week's supply, I thought. And three days at the most, if this weather kept on the way it was going.

I couldn't remember when Gus Tyson had been here last. It seemed like, for a while, he was here every night, talking and drinking coffee with Mom. But now, looking at the woodpile, I realized that it had been some time since we'd seen Gus.

The stewing hen was bubbling on the front lid of the stove, and Mom was stirring a batch of dumplings to the right consistency to drop into the broth.

Mom turned to look at me as I crowded close to the stove to get warm. "As soon as I get off work tomorrow, I'll go get a coat for you. Wearing nothing but that sweater and a cotton dress," she said, "you'll be coming down with pneumonia."

"We'll all have pneumonia if Gus doesn't get here soon with a load of wood. There's only a skeleton of a woodpile left now."

"You let me worry about heating this house," Mom said sharply. "I'm talking now of keeping you two kids warm on the way to school and back this winter. Getting you decent coats like the other kids are wearing . . ." Her words trailed off.

With an angry flip of her wrist, Mom began to drop

dumplings into the pot of chicken and broth, slapping the spoon smartly on the rim of the kettle to dislodge the dough, then dipping another dumpling.

I didn't mention Gus Tyson or the wood again. I knew it worried Mom to have him bringing wood when she couldn't pay for it. She had said so time after time. But I wondered how she could afford to buy Robert and me a coat when she couldn't pay for the wood.

I wanted to tell Mom that it didn't matter whether I had a coat like the other kids were wearing. I'd rather wear my old sweater and freeze my butt off than to wear a coat and be like them. But in her state of mind right now, it wouldn't be wise.

I wiped the table and set three places for dinner, putting a cup and saucer at Mom's place for coffee.

"Seely, put out two more cups," Mom said quietly. "I've got cocoa heating on the back of the stove for you and Robert."

I turned quickly to get two more cups and saucers. Hot cocoa was a rare treat, saved for special occasions. And this was just an ordinary Sunday.

"I thought a hot drink would take the chill off," Mom said, as if she knew what I'd been thinking. "After that cold walk to church and back, you both need it."

At the dinner table, Mom brought up the walk to church again. "We ought to look around for a church closer to home," she said. "One that holds an evening service that I could go to."

Robert gave me a look and made a face. "Go to church twice a day?"

He didn't try to hide his aversion to this new notion of

Mom's. And though I felt much the same way that Robert did, I didn't say so. I figured that Mom had made up her mind to it, or she wouldn't have mentioned it. By this time next week we'd probably be going to church with Nedra Noyer, instead of out in the country with the Hollises.

The only thing I could think of that was worse than being the new kid in school was walking into a strange church where nobody knew me. But if Mom said we were going, we'd go. And she would be the one to say.

After dinner, Mom had mending to do and went to her room. Robert and I cleaned up the kitchen. Robert said, "Why do I always have to dry the dishes?" So for a change, he washed the dishes. I dried and put them away. When the kitchen was neat and clean, Robert went to look for thin boards suitable for stretching hides. I went to the loft room.

As I did every Sunday afternoon, I wrote to Julie. I told her that Mom was buying new coats for Robert and me, making it sound like we were doing better than we were. And I gave her a list of my grades. All A's but one. I never could understand Algebra, I told her. I didn't mention that my hands were a mess and the kids at school avoided me as if I had leprosy. It would make Julie unhappy, and she couldn't do anything about it.

I brought my diary up to date. I hadn't written in it for a few days, and I had a lot of catching up to do. When I could find nothing more to write about, I got the jar of mutton tallow salve and dosed my hands with it.

The loft room was usually the warmest room in the

house, but now that I wasn't writing, I felt the chill up here. I had forgotten to feed the stove before I came upstairs, and it had probably gone out completely.

I hurried downstairs and opened the firebox. There were enough live coals on the grates that by adding kindling a little at a time, I could bring the fire alive. When Robert came in from the shed with his hide boards, I had a fair-sized fire going in the cookstove.

Robert pulled a chair up close to the woodbox and started whittling the boards he had brought into the house, rounding off the ends and smoothing the sides so the animal skins would stretch over them. He was making a mess with the flying shavings that missed the woodbox. I yelled at him for it.

"I'll clean it up," he yelled back. "It's too cold to do this in the shed."

"You kids stop your bickering, Seely," Mom called from her room.

Robert gave me a smug look and went right on whittling.

The wind had dropped during the night, and Monday morning was clear, cold, and still. The kind of day that will freeze you in your tracks, Robert said, if you don't keep moving. I ran to the privy and back so fast that I didn't have time to feel the cold.

Mom had left a note on the table telling Robert and me to dress warm, come straight home from school, and stay here.

Robert read the note and said, "But I'm supposed to run the trapline with Dustin this evening."

"Tell him you'll do it tomorrow," I said. "Mom said to stay home today."

Robert put a flannel shirt on over his pajama top, then slipped his sweater on over it all. "It's only for one day," he said, tugging at the sweater to stretch it. "I'll have a coat to wear tomorrow."

Seemed like everything we needed or wanted was always a day away.

"Don't set your heart on a new coat, little brother," I said. "Mom wants us each to have one, but she may find they are out of her reach. So don't say anything, if we don't get coats."

Robert's eyes got wide, like he was going to cry. "We'll manage with what we've got," I said, buttoning his sweater up close to his chin.

I put on the faded denim jacket that I'd worn last year over my sweater, and we left for school. Robert put his hands in his pockets to keep warm. I crossed my arms over my chest and slipped my hands into my jacket sleeves. I wished that I could hide them there for the rest of the day.

At the grade school, I told Robert to wait inside for me this afternoon and not stand outside in the cold. Then I went slowly toward the high school. I wanted to be the last one to enter the schoolhouse today. I had enough to contend with, without having to explain why I was wearing a boy's blue denim jacket.

I reached into my desk for my biology book, workbook, pencil, and paper, just as the bell rang for our first class. I got up and followed the rest of the juniors down the hall to the homeroom. I took the seat assigned to me on the first day of school. The last desk, in the last row of seats.

Hoping to get rid of the smell of mutton tallow, I had washed myself good before I left home. But instead of washing the smell away, it seemed to have spread from my hands to the rest of me. As the room got warmer, the scent of the ointment became stronger. I put my hands in my lap, but I could still smell it.

Arvella Simpson raised her hand for permission to speak. Mr. Gibbs nodded his head.

"May I please change seats?" she asked. "Seely smells bad."

"Then change seats with Virgil," Mr. Gibbs told her.

Arvella stood up to move to the other end of the row, but Virgil wouldn't budge. "I don't want to sit next to Seely," he said.

Mr. Gibbs looked at me. "Seely, what seems to be your problem?"

"It's the salve on my hands. It has a funny smell."

He motioned for me to come to his desk. "Let me see," he said, taking both my hands in his. He looked closely at my hands, then raised them toward his face. "Mutton tallow," he said, dropping my hands. "I've used it myself."

After he sent me back to my seat, Mr. Gibbs was silent for a moment, waiting for the room to grow quiet, then he spoke to the class.

"The smell you have found so offensive," he said, "is an ointment that has been in use since your great-grandfather's day. Because of its main ingredient, the ointment is known as mutton tallow salve."

He looked around the room as if to assure himself that he had everyone's attention. "Your assignment for next Monday will be to bring to class a complete list of the other ingredients used to make this salve," he said. "We could use that as our group project, and perhaps make a small supply for the school," he added.

As moans and groans rose from the class, Mr. Gibbs smiled. "The subject is closed," he said. "Let us get back to today's lesson."

Mr. Gibbs turned to write on the blackboard, and Ellis Van Waggoner whispered, "Seely, what have you got us into now?" But it was said in a friendly manner, with a smile to go with it.

No one mentioned the scent of the salve for the rest of the day. And it wasn't because the odor of mutton had faded. Whenever I stood near a heat register I could still smell it.

I didn't have to wait for Deidre after school. She was in the cloakroom when I went to get my jacket.

"Is that the only coat you've got to wear," she asked, as I slipped the denim jacket over my sweater.

I thought of Mom's promise to get me a coat today. If not today, I reasoned, it would be soon. "My coat is at the cleaners," I replied shortly and started out of the building.

"Seely, don't walk so fast," Deidre said. "I want to ask a favor of you."

"Ask me while we walk," I said. "I told Robert to stay at the school till I got there, and he's been waiting alone for an hour now."

"He won't be alone," Deidre said. "Dustin will be

with him. The boys were going to check their traps after school, so Robert probably didn't wait."

I was already put out with Deidre Hollis for the way she had turned up her nose at my jacket, but to hear her dispute my word about Robert waiting for me was too much. Robert wouldn't leave the school when he knew I was expecting him to be there.

"Robert will be there," I replied sharply. "Maybe Dustin has gone home. Robert can't go trapping today. He was told not to leave the house."

We walked wide apart, in silence, to the grade school, where Robert and Dustin both were waiting for us.

Deidre and Dustin Hollis didn't stay long at our house. Dustin took the hide boards that Robert had shaped for him and took off toward the woods to check the traps. Deidre left at the same time. She never did say what the favor was that she wanted from me.

"Seely," Robert said. "Is it a lie, if you say in your mind that it will be true later on?"

"Robert, what are you talking about?"

"Well, at noon today," he said, "I wouldn't go outside to play. The teacher asked me, didn't I have a coat, and I told her I did. Is that a lie?"

"If it's a lie," I replied gently, "I've got a bigger one to top it. I told Deidre that my coat was at the cleaners."

Robert started to smile and, when I smiled back, it spread all over his face.

chapter twelve

Supper was over, and Robert and I were trying on the new coats that Mom had brought home in a brown Salvation Army bag. Robert's coat was a brown plaid mackinaw that fit like it had been made for him. And it looked to be almost brand new.

The coat Mom had brought for me was a plain tan wraparound. A loose belt was all that held it together in front. I put it on, tied the belt, and slid my hands into the side pockets. The sleeves were the right length, but the coat felt large enough for two people my size, I told Mom.

She turned up the wide collar, and drew the coat lapels across my chest. "It's supposed to fit loose," Mom said and stood back to look at me. "Straighten up, Seely, and that coat will look fine. Once I get it cleaned and pressed," she added.

I took it off and laid it on the ironing board beside the mackinaw, to be pressed with a damp cloth.

"Nedra Noyer said she thought someone had paid a pretty price for that coat when it was new," Mom said, fingering the fabric. "And I'd say they got their money's worth."

"This sudden cold snap caught Nedra's young'uns without warm things too," Mom went on. "When I mentioned that I was looking to buy you kids coats, she said she'd go to the store with me."

Mom paused and shook her head. "Nedra must have spent every bit of five dollars in there, getting coats and caps and sweaters for her brood."

She didn't say how much she had spent on our coats.

Mom touched a finger to her tongue, then to the iron to test its heat. When the spit sizzled against the hot iron, I got a pan of water and the pressing cloth. "I can press the coats," I said, as I reached for the mackinaw.

Mom took the coat from my hand and spread it inside out on the ironing board. "Seely, go dose your hands and leave the ironing to me." She sounded testy, as if I had tried her patience to the limit.

It seemed to me that since Mom had worked all day and bought the coats, the least I could do would be to get them ready to wear.

"I only wanted to help," I said.

"You do your part around here," Mom said.

I thought she was finished with me. I started to the loft room to dose my hands. But Mom had more to say.

"Seely, the hardest thing in the world is to learn to accept things." Mom flipped the mackinaw over on the ironing board. "I don't mean acceptance of the way things are," she said. "I think we've all learned that by now. But, Seely, I'm saying that you can't be the giver every time. Always doing for others, yet not letting them do for you."

Mom set the iron on end and gave the jacket a vigorous shake. After she had looked it over, she handed it to Robert to hang up in the other room.

She picked up my coat and ran her fingers along the seams like a tailor checking his work for flaws.

"I did the best I could for you, Seely," Mom said, almost as if she was apologizing to me. "I hope when I get this coat done up, you won't be ashamed to wear it."

As Mom turned to lay the coat on the ironing board, I did something that I hadn't done in a long time. I crossed the room and kissed her.

"I'm not ashamed to wear it," I said. "I like it."

I did like the coat. I liked the way I felt when I belted it around my waist. And the way the hem brushed against the back of my legs with a little swish when I walked. I couldn't let it matter that it had been worn before I got it. I needed a coat, and Mom had provided me with the best she could afford.

"Robert's gone on to bed," Mom said, breaking into my thoughts. "You'd better tend to your hands now."

I said, "Mom, what's in that salve I use, besides the mutton tallow?"

"I used to know," Mom said thoughtfully. "Seems to

93

me it has camphor gum or turpentine, but I couldn't say. Why do you ask?"

"It's a project in Biology class," I said. "We're going to try to make it for the school."

"Then you'd better ask old Mr. Hollis. He could probably tell you. Those old folks grew up making their own salve and soap, and whatever else they needed."

"I thought I'd ask Gus Tyson when he brought the wood. He ought to know how it is made."

Mom turned away to check the lock on the back door. "You'd do better to see Grandpa Hollis. There's no telling when Gus Tyson will make it to town again."

She didn't look at me as she said, "Go to bed now. It's late."

I went to the loft room, and a few minutes later the light went out downstairs. I got into my nightgown, then I sat on the side of my bed and rubbed the salve into my hands. Bad as I hated the stinking stuff, I had to admit it was healing my hands.

The next morning, as we were getting ready for school, Robert said, "I hope it doesn't get too warm today for my mackinaw."

"You'd do well to wish it would get warm," I said.

"If this cold spell lasts very long, we'll run out of firewood."

"No, we won't," Robert said positively. "Gus Tyson wouldn't allow that to happen."

I didn't feel that sure about it. Our woodpile had never been as low as it was now. And from the way Mom had talked last night, we weren't likely to see Gus Tyson anytime soon.

In case Mom got home before we did, I left a note on

the table to let her know that Robert and I were going to the Hollises, to find out about the salve from Grandpa Hollis.

I think Robert and I were the first ones on the street that morning. We were that anxious to try out our new used coats.

On mornings when Deidre and Dustin were running late, they would take the shortcut to school instead of calling for us. We never waited for them if they didn't show up. This was one of those days.

I was waiting for Deidre when she got to school. I had a favor to ask of her today.

"Would it be all right for Robert and me to go home with you after school today?"

We were walking down the hall toward the assembly. Deidre stopped dead still and looked at me with surprise. "What a silly question, Seely. Of course it's all right." She took my arm, and we went on. "You are welcome at our house at any time," she said.

Robert and Dustin had gone on home as soon as their school was out. They had been at the Hollises for an hour or more when Deidre and I got there. As we crossed the yard toward the house, the boys came out of the barn and called to us.

"Hey, Seely," Robert said. "Come and see the muskrat skins that Dustin got out of the traps last night."

"I'll see them later. After I've talked to Grandpa Hollis." I went on toward the house.

"I wouldn't go in there yet," Dustin said. "Mom and Grandpa are fussing again."

"What started it this time?" Deidre asked wryly. "You or me?"

95

Dustin gave her a slight grin. "Neither one of us," he said. "It was a bird."

"A bird?" Deidre said. "I don't believe it!"

"God's truth." Dustin held up his right hand. "A bird flew into the house," he said, "and Mom had to chase it all over before she could get it out the door.

"Grandpa Hollis said it was bad luck for a bird to fly loose in the house," Dustin went on. "And Mom told him that it was bad luck for the bird. If she could catch it, she'd kill it."

Deidre said that since the fight didn't concern her or Dustin, we could go on in. "You can ask Grandpa how to make that salve," she said, "and he'll forget to fuss at Mom. He'll have something else to think on."

When Deidre and I walked into the kitchen, with Robert and Dustin close behind us, Grandpa Hollis was saying, "If my wife, Ariet was here, she'd tell you there is going to be a death in this family."

"She always believed if a bird flew against the window-pane, there would be a death," Mersy corrected him.

Grandpa Hollis got more upset than he was already. "I knew her a sight longer than you did," he shouted. "I guess I know what she said."

Mersy sniffed and turned her back on him. We spoke to her as we filed across the room and moved quietly out of their way. I think Mrs. Hollis forgot we were there, the moment we passed from her sight. I doubt that Grandpa even saw us come in.

"When my uncle Henry died," he said to Mersy's back, "a bird came right into this house and stayed here until he died three days later."

"I'm not surprised," Mrs. Hollis muttered under her breath. "The poor thing probably starved to death."

But Grandpa Hollis heard her. He hit the table with his ham-sized fist. "I'm saying that my uncle Henry died," he shouted. "Not the damn bird!"

When she saw how excited the old man was getting, Mersy Hollis tried to mollify him. She said that Grandma Hollis had been a superstitious woman. Uncle Henry would have died had there never been a bird within a mile of the place. But instead of soothing his anger, her words seemed to add fuel to the fire. He got even more defensive.

"Are you calling my wife and me liars?" he demanded to know. "We know what happened. We were there, you weren't."

"Well," Mersy said, turning away, and supposedly giving in to him, "if anyone dies, we'll know it was because of that bird."

While Grandpa Hollis was momentarily at a loss for words, Dustin walked up to the old man and touched him to get his attention.

"Grandpa," Dustin said. "We need your help on a problem we're having at school."

Mr. Hollis turned at once and put his arm around Dustin's shoulders, guiding him toward the table. Grandpa Hollis sat down. Then he motioned impatiently for the rest of us to sit with him.

"Well, son. Where's your book?"

"It's not that kind of problem, Grandpa. We need to know something."

Mr. Hollis stroked his beard thoughtfully as he looked

in turn at each of us. Then he asked softly, for our ears only, "Are you in trouble at school?"

Dustin shook his head no. Then he took one of my hands and held it close to the old man's face. "Grandpa, do you know what that smell is?"

Grandpa Hollis pushed my hand away from his face. Then he yelled at Dustin. "Good Lord, son! Don't ever shove mutton tallow into a man's face like that!"

Dustin grinned at him. "Did you ever make mutton tallow salve, Grandpa?"

"More times than there's fingers and toes on the four of you," he replied.

"Would you tell me how to make it?" I asked.

He looked at me, combing his beard with his fingers as he considered it. "How much do you figure to make?" he asked.

"It's for Biology class," I said. "The teacher said that we had to find out how to make mutton tallow salve before we came to class on Monday."

"Then get your pencil and paper ready," Grandpa Hollis told me. "I'll tell you how to make it, but mind you, don't ever bring me any of that stuff."

I had never heard of most of the ingredients that Grandpa Hollis reeled off his tongue as easily as I could recite how to make pancakes. Besides the mutton tallow, there was balm of Gilead buds, white pine gum, red precipitate, soap, sugar, and sweet oil. "You can always use butter in place of the sweet oil," he said. "But butter goes rancid if you keep it too long."

Deidre had been right when she said that her grandpa would forget to fight with her mother if he had us kids to talk to. He sat at the table, speaking softly of the olden days, the times he had known. In them days, he said, even a boy of Robert's age knew how to make a poultice or set a broken bone.

"That's no reflection on you, son," he said to Robert. "There's just no call for it nowadays."

Mersy Hollis lit a lamp and set it in the middle of the table. I blinked at the sudden light as if coming awake. I hadn't realized how long we had been sitting there listening to Grandpa Hollis's stories. It was beginning to get dark outside, and Robert and I still had chores to do when we got home.

I stood up and beckoned to Robert. "I thank you for your help, Mr. Hollis." I put out my hand to shake his. Then I thought better of it and let my hand drop. "I sure do appreciate it," I said.

Grandpa Hollis got up, took my hand, and shook it. "You are welcome, young lady," he said and kind of bowed his head to me.

Later on the way home Robert said, "Seely, do you know why Grandpa and Mrs. Hollis fight all the time?"

I told him what Deidre had told me. She said that her mother blamed Grandpa Hollis because he hadn't put his foot down and kept their dad from leaving them. "But that was years ago," I said. "I don't think they're still fighting about that."

"I don't either," Robert replied.

A little further up the road, Robert said, "Dustin told me that he would run away from home, if it wasn't for his grandpa."

"He wouldn't have a home to run away from," I said,

"if it wasn't for his grandpa. They live in his house, eat his food, and they live off the money that Grandpa Hollis gets for renting his land out to the farmers."

"Seely, how do you know they do?"

"Dustin told me so, the day we set traps together."

Robert didn't say anything more until we had turned off the Bottom Road, and we saw the light shining from the windows of our house. For once, Mom was home ahead of us.

"I'm sure glad we don't have to depend on anyone else for a place to live," Robert said. "Mom would be as cranky as Mrs. Hollis if she had to feel obligated for every bite and the roof over her head."

We cut across the backyard to go through the lean-to shed. About ten steps inside the shed door, Robert and I both stopped and stared at what lay before us. It was still light enough in the shed to see the kitchen steps and the high mound of lump coal that was piled to the very edge of them.

chapter thirteen

*R*obert took the steps to the kitchen two at a time and burst into the room where Mom was fixing supper.

"What's that coal doing in the shed?" he gasped out.

"We're going to burn it in the stoves," Mom replied evenly. "Everyone uses coal in the city."

"But why do we have to?" Robert argued. "Gus Tyson will be here any day now with a load of wood."

"Gus Tyson is not coming back here." Mom spoke firmly, but patiently. "I told him, when he wouldn't take pay for that last load of wood, not to ever come back with another one. It was getting so I dreaded the sight of that truck coming down the alley."

"That doesn't mean that we won't see Gus," I said to placate Robert. "He'll be back. Gus is our friend."

"It had to stop," Mom said. "Seely, you're old enough to understand why I couldn't go on taking favors from Gus Tyson, having him believe that one day—" Mom stopped abruptly and turned back to her cooking.

Robert and I went quietly out of the room to hang up our coats.

Later, when supper was over and the chores were all done, Mom said, "It doesn't seem possible that we're coming on to December, and it's time to stock up on food stuff again. You kids come to the hotel, when you get out of school Friday, and help me carry home the groceries."

Then Mom asked had I got what I needed from Mr. Hollis, and I replied that I had.

"Grandpa Hollis and Mersy were having cross words when we got there," I said. "I didn't have a chance to speak to him about the salve, right away. That's why we were so late getting home."

"Were they fussing because you kids were there?"

At the same time that I said, "No. It was over a bird," Robert said, "Mrs. Hollis picks on Grandpa because she doesn't like to feel beholden to him for every bite she puts in her mouth."

A look of understanding crossed Robert's face. He clapped a hand over his mouth, as if to stop the very thought of being indebted to anyone for anything from entering the room.

That was only one of the reasons why Mom refused to accept firewood as a gift from Gus Tyson, I thought. I was sure I knew the other reason too. Mom's fine auburn hair was laced with white, but she still stood tall and slim as a girl. And Gus Tyson, a widower for many years, couldn't miss seeing the warmth, and sometimes the fire, in her clear, dark brown eyes and believe that after a time Mom would come to look on him as more than a good friend.

It was hard to get used to burning coal in the cookstove. I missed the clean smell of wood smoke on cold mornings. And I missed Gus Tyson. But I learned to live without his friendly visits, and I tried my level best not to choke and gag on the coal smoke.

When I complained about the coal dust, Mom said I would get used to it. Everyone else had lived through it, she said. No one burned wood in Bedford nowadays. I could believe it. The white limestone buildings were soot-streaked from the black coal smoke. When it rained, water ran black and gritty off the roof into our rain-barrel.

Banked fires would explode during the night from coal gasses trapped in the stove. The next morning, there would be a film of black dust on everything in the house. Mom didn't seem to notice the dust. At least, she didn't remark on it.

I suppose it could have been that Mom didn't see the coal soot. She was gone before daylight every day, and she didn't get back until after dark. By that time, I had the house cleaned.

On Friday before Thanksgiving, we were supposed to meet Mom at the hotel to go buy groceries. Robert found all kinds of excuses not to go with me. He teased all the way to school to be allowed to go home with Dustin.

"You know the way to the hotel," Robert said. "You don't need me to lead you. And I've never yet got to run the trapline with Dustin."

He was right. There was no need for him to go with me except I didn't like to walk to town by myself.

Finally, I said he could go home with Dustin. "Maybe Deidre can walk to the hotel with me," I said.

But Deidre had chores to do at home. "If I'd known beforehand," she said, "I could have gone with you."

Just then, Virgil Rowe went by on his way out of the school. "Seely, walk downwind from me," he said, "and I'll go anywhere with you."

"Virgil, you dumb snerd," Deidre called after him. But he just laughed and went on out the door.

"Pay him no mind, Seely," she said. "I can't even smell that salve today."

I told Deidre that it didn't bother me what anyone said. But it did. And she knew it. I said a quick goodbye to Deidre and went on my way.

There was hardly anyone on the streets at this time, but I kept my eyes straight ahead, never looking down or around, until I had turned down the alley beside the hotel. I was heading for the back door of the hotel, when I stumped my toe on a rise in the ground, stumbled, and barely caught myself. "If that had been a briar," I grumbled aloud, "I would've jumped over it!"

Someone laughed, and I turned quickly. I had thought myself alone in the alley. In the dusky twilight, between the tall buildings, I saw a young man standing in the doorway to the hotel. I would have to pass by him to get inside to meet Mom.

"You must be Mrs. Robinson's girl, Seely," he said,

104

stepping to one side to open the door for me. "She said you'd be here about now."

I ducked my chin farther into my coat collar and walked by him into the hotel. He put his hand on my arm and matched his steps to mine.

"I'm Arlo Hawks," he said. "I kind of work here with your mother."

"Then you see more of her than I do," I replied shortly.

He missed a step and dropped his hand from my arm. "I guess I do at that," he said.

In the bright light of the hotel kitchen, I took a long look at Arlo Hawks. He was taller than I'd thought and thin as a bean pole. His sandy hair grew long and curled over his neck and ears.

"Well, what do you think?'" he asked. "Will I do?"

I felt myself blush, and I looked away. I liked the way Arlo Hawks spoke, his hazel eyes and thin face, but I couldn't tell him that. "You're too skinny," I said. "You couldn't make a good shadow."

He laughed, took my arm again, and led me to the room where Mom was waiting.

Arlo Hawks was holding onto me like he had just bought and paid for the privilege, but Mom didn't seem to notice it. Her glance went on by me. "Where's Robert?" she asked sharply.

Robert was well able to take care of himself, but Mom refused to believe it. She still considered Robert a child, and she held me responsible for him.

"Robert didn't want to come with me," I said. "He and Dustin had other things to do."

Mom said, "Humph," and got her coat and scarf and

105

put them on. "It's going to be pitch dark before we get our trading done," she said, heading for the door.

I knotted my coat belt snug around me, stuck my hands in the pockets, and turned to follow Mom out of the hotel.

"Mrs. Robinson," Arlo Hawks called from the hotel door, "would it be all right if I came to your house on Sunday?"

Mom seemed surprised at his request, but she granted it quickly. "You're welcome, Arlo," she said. "Come early and have a bite of dinner with us."

Arlo smiled and waved a hand to take in both Mom and me, then he turned back inside, out of the cold wind.

I hoped my face didn't show my surprise at Mom inviting a strange boy to eat with us. She just didn't do things like that. We had known Deidre and Dustin for months now, and she had never asked them over for a meal.

"That boy could stand a few good meals," Mom said, as if she knew what I was thinking. "I doubt that he has anything to eat except the one meal that comes with his job as a busboy. And it is a wonder to me how he keeps that," she added.

"What's wrong with Arlo Hawks? Won't he work?"

"Oh, he's a good worker," Mom said. "But didn't you see the black grime around his fingernails? Arlo fancies himself to be a mechanic. When he's not bussing dishes at the hotel, he is fooling around with automobiles at Ray's garage."

I hadn't noticed Arlo Hawks's hands. I was too aware

of my own hands, and trying to keep them out of sight, to look at anyone else's.

I had expected Mom to raise cain with me for not bringing Robert, but she didn't say a word about it. She went on talking about her work and the other people at the hotel. I didn't know them, but I listened in case she mentioned Arlo Hawks.

While Mom talked, I let my mind wander ahead to Sunday, when I would see Arlo again. Maybe he would be the someone I could go out with. Seemed like every girl in the junior class, except me, had a boyfriend. Even Arvella Simpson had a boy to walk out with. Not that I would want just any boy. Certainly not one that I had seen at school. But Arlo Hawks was different. He was a man living alone and holding down two jobs.

I had thought, when Dustin took my hand that day, that perhaps I had found a boyfriend. But Dustin hadn't seen me in the same light. In his eyes, I was just Robert's sister and Deidre's friend. But, for a while, that didn't keep me from dreaming about him and seeing him as the handsomest boy alive.

Now, Dustin's face and figure had become as familiar to me as my brother Robert's. And just about as interesting. I liked Dustin, but he was a far cry from what I had in mind for a boyfriend.

By the time Mom and I had reached the lights of the grocery store, my mind had gone full circle and I was back to thinking of Arlo Hawks again. Arlo wasn't as handsome as Dustin, but he had a certain charm about him. I hugged my coat close around me and smiled to myself.

"Seely, pay attention!" Mom shook my arm. "Didn't you hear what I said?"

I cast back in my mind, fishing for a clue to the last words I had heard Mom say, and I came up empty. "I'm sorry," I said. "I guess I was thinking of something else."

"Your mind is always somewhere else," she said, as if stating a proven fact. "I asked if you'd made a list of the staples we need."

I gave her the grocery list I had made out before I had left for school, and she read quickly through the items. "Raisins?" Mom looked at me, and I could tell she was erasing that. "We have no use for raisins, Seely."

"You could make a pie," I said. "We haven't had a raisin pie in ages. And besides," I added, "we ought to fix a little extra for Sunday, with Arlo Hawks coming to eat with us."

Mom dismissed Arlo with a wave of her hand. "Arlo Hawks is nobody special," she said. "He'll eat whatever we put on the table and be glad to get it, no doubt."

But Mom bought the raisins for a pie. I guess her pride wouldn't allow her to do less than the best she could afford. Not even for a nobody like Arlo Hawks.

When Mom and I walked into the kitchen at home, Robert and Dustin were playing checkers. Dustin jumped to take the grocery bags out of Mom's hands, and Robert cleared a space on the table for me to set mine.

"We've got supper ready to eat," Robert said, as Mom took off her coat and reached for an apron. "Dustin caught two rabbits in the traps yesterday, and Mrs. Hollis cooked them. She said it was no trouble at all." Robert barely paused for breath. "She was baking bread, and she put the rabbits in the oven and baked them at the same time. She gave me a loaf of hot bread to bring home too," he added.

Mom smiled at Robert. "I hope you thanked Mrs. Hollis," she said.

When he nodded in reply, Mom turned to Dustin. "How is your mother these days?"

"Mom is fine," Dustin replied. "She's still trying to get the best of Grandpa."

"And how is your grandpa?"

"Same as always." He grinned. "Ornery as a sack of snakes and tough as a turkey buzzard. He was complaining today of his rheumatism. He accused Mom of swinging the door open and letting in the cold wind just to irritate his aching bones."

Mom shook her head and didn't comment on that.

"We didn't run the traps this evening," Dustin said, as he got ready to leave. "Robert was afraid he'd ruin his good coat. But if you don't mind, we'll go down the trapline tomorrow, when there is plenty of daylight."

Mom said that sounded wise to her. As long as Robert got his chores done before he went gallivanting through the woods, she didn't mind. "And you boys be careful of those steel traps," she said.

Dustin said, "I'll look out for Robert, Mrs. Robinson. There will be no reason for him to even touch one of the traps."

In my mind I could see the evil-looking contraptions that I had helped to stake out in the woods. I wondered what the boys could find so fascinating about them. But ever since Dustin first spoke of trapping to Robert, he could think of nothing else. I looked across the room at Robert's wide-eyed, innocent face, and I wished he had never heard of trapping animals.

.

chapter fourteen

*I*t was raining when Dustin came Saturday afternoon to get Robert to go run the traplines. I couldn't say no. Mom had already given her consent.

I had finished the week's washing, and wet clothes were hanging all over the house to dry. We had a big fire going in both the stoves, but the room still felt cold and damp.

Dustin looked at the wet clothes hanging from the wire across the front of the balcony and laughed. "Seely, that is what I call using your noggin."

"Mom is going to kill her for hanging things up there," Robert said.

"I couldn't very well hang them outside," I said. "Not in the rain. Besides," I added, "everything will be dry and put away before Mom ever gets home."

Dustin said he had hardly noticed the rain. It had slacked off to a drizzle by the time he got here. "But it wouldn't do any harm to wrap up good," he told Robert.

Robert went to the front part of the house to get bundled up against the weather. I turned to Dustin to ask him and Deidre to come and eat dinner with us tomorrow. "A fellow who works with Mom at the hotel is coming to dinner," I said. And Dustin interrupted me with a whoop.

"Your mom's got herself a boyfriend!" He whooped again, and his smile spread from ear to ear.

I felt like smacking the silly smile around to the back of his head. "Don't be ridiculous," I said. "He is just a boy who works at the hotel. And besides," I added angrily, "what makes you think that my mom would have a boyfriend?"

"Heck, Seely, I didn't aim to make you mad. But when a man comes to dinner with a widow woman"—he smiled sheepishly—"a fellow just naturally thinks . . ."

"This widow has two kids," I snapped at him. "Did you think of that?"

Dustin stared at me as if he had never seen me before, and I glared at him. Then Robert came into the room wearing my old denim jacket, with Jamie's blue stocking cap pulled over his ears, and I turned on him. "Who gave you permission to wear my things?"

Robert's eyes got wide, and he took a step back from

me. "Seely, I've worn these things lots of times, and you never cared. Why are you so mad about it now?"

"Oh, Robert," I said, "I'm sorry. I don't care if you wear those old things." I looked from one boy to the other. "I started to ask Dustin could he and Deidre come to dinner tomorrow because this boy Mom works with was going to be here. Then all of a sudden we were fighting, and I don't even know why I got mad."

Robert turned to Dustin. "Do you know why she is mad?"

Dustin shook his head. "We were just talking," he said.

"Are you and Deidre coming over tomorrow?"

He kind of grinned at Robert, then he turned to me. "That is up to Seely," Dustin said. "Whatever she says."

"We don't know Arlo Hawks," I said quietly. "Please come over to keep us company."

Dustin put on his gloves, and he and Robert went to the back door. I thought he was going to leave without a word to me. But as he opened the door, Dustin said, "Seely, you can count on Deidre and me being here in time for dinner."

I had beans cooking for supper. When Robert got back, I would make dumplings to drop in the bean broth. Mom would eat supper at the hotel tonight, as she always did when she was working late. And we could eat whenever we got hungry.

Until the clothes got dry, all I had to do was to dust the furniture and keep the fires going. I put a few lumps of coal in each stove and got out the furniture polish and cloth. Since there was no one there but me to be bothered by the smell of mutton tallow, I got the jar of salve and rubbed a good-sized dollop into both hands. Then I put socks over my hands like gloves, so I wouldn't smear it on anything.

I don't know how many times I had fired up the stoves, or how long I had been polishing tables and chairs, but it didn't seem like any time at all when Robert walked in the back door.

He went right by me and threw himself face down on the daybed. I took the socks off my hands and dropped them with the dust cloth, then I went over to his bed.

"What's the matter, Robert? Did you hurt yourself?"

He moved his head on the pillow, but he didn't answer me.

Robert had left his overshoes in the shed, but he still had on his cap and jacket. I slipped the cap from his head and smoothed his hair. "Talk to me, little brother," I said quietly. "What's wrong with you?"

"I'm sick at my stomach." He turned his head to look at me. "Seely, I got sick at my stomach."

His face was white, like dough, with a hurt, pinched look to it. I could believe he was sick, but I couldn't figure out why. He had been fine when he left the house with Dustin Hollis.

"Let me take this damp jacket," I said, turning him to unbutton the front. "Then I'll make you some hot cocoa."

Robert sat up long enough to get his arms out of the jacket, then he lay back down with his face in his arms. I put a blanket over him, then I went to the kitchen to make the cocoa.

Most of the time, Robert behaved so grown up that we

had a tendency to treat him as a grownup, forgetting that he was only ten years old. And that was the way he wanted it. But now that he was sick, he seemed much younger than his age.

I washed my hands in hot sudsy water and put a few drops of clove oil on them to take away the scent of the salve. The clove oil smarted and stung for a while, but the sweet scent of the cloves was worth it.

I was pouring a cup of cocoa to take to Robert when I heard someone coming up the back steps. I set the cup on the table and went to open the door.

Old Mr. Hollis stood on the top step, his hat in one hand, his cane in the other. "I've come to see the boy," he said.

I swung the door wide open. "Robert is in the front room," I said. "Go on in and make yourself at home."

Grandpa Hollis smoothed at his shock of white hair and beard, then he went slowly to where Robert lay face down on the bed. The old man drew a chair up close to the bed and began to speak to Robert.

"Son," he said gently, "won't you face me while we are talking?" When Robert didn't move or make a sound, Grandpa Hollis went on speaking. "I've come here today to tell you that I was a-miss when I was teaching you trapping, and I'm sorry. But dang it all, boy, I thought you knew that the critters had to be killed once they're trapped! I'll grant you," he went on, "it is not a pretty sight to see a raccoon clubbed to death. But it had to be done. It would have been cruel to free a crippled animal. The other animals would have killed him later," Grandpa Hollis added.

I offered Robert the cocoa, and he sat on the edge of

the daybed to take it, his knees touching the old man's knees. I asked Mr. Hollis could I bring him something to drink. "I'd not turn down a cup of that bean broth I smell," he said. I brought him a cup of it. Then I left him and Robert to their talking. Trapping animals had not turned out to be what Robert had expected.

I could hear the sound of their voices, while I was taking the clothes from the line on the balcony, but not what they were saying. I was ready to start the ironing when Mr. Hollis brought his cup to the kitchen and said he had to be starting back home.

I thanked him for coming to see Robert and asked him to come again. "Robert has learned a lot from you," I said. "And there is a lot more for him to find out about."

Grandpa Hollis ducked his head to me. "Aye, girl," he said, "you can dress a boy up, but you can't take him to town."

He opened the door and started down the back steps. Before he reached the bottom step, I said, "What did you mean by that?"

Grandpa Hollis stepped to the ground. Then he turned and looked at me. "Girl, I can teach that boy everything I know," he said. "But there are things he has to find out for himself. Every man has to do his own thinking and feeling and making up his own mind. I can't do that for him."

He studied my face for a moment, then he touched his hand to his hat and turned away. I stood in the door and watched until he reached the alley and started slowly toward the Bottom Road. I thought that was a long walk for an old man to make, just to comfort a boy.

I started ironing the few pieces that needed pressing, so I could get it out of the way before supper. Robert came to the kitchen with his cap and jacket and reached for the coal bucket.

"I'll bring in the coal," he said. "Then we can talk while you get supper ready."

While Robert was doing his chores, I made dumplings and dropped them in the bean soup. Then, while they were cooking, I put the ironing away. By the time Robert had washed the coal dust off his hands, supper was ready.

"Robert," I said, "do you want to talk now?"

He got a sick look on his face. "Not while we are eating," he said.

Later, while we were waiting for Mom to get home, Robert said, "I won't be trapping with Dustin anymore. Grandpa Hollis said that I would be more help working with him on the furs."

"Robert, you don't know a thing about curing furs."

"That's what I told him. But Grandpa Hollis says it is real simple. He'll teach me."

"It may seem simple to him," I said. "He has been handling furs all his life. But are you sure you can handle animal pelts and not get sick again?"

Robert looked earnestly at me. "Seely, for a share of the money those furs will bring, I'll not get so sick that I can't do my work."

We sat quietly for a moment, then Robert went on to explain how he would work with Grandpa Hollis.

"Grandpa Hollis has got a pumice rock, and he'll catch the rainwater to wash the skins," he said. "But I'll do the washing and scraping. Grandpa has got rheumatism in his hands so bad that he can't do that. And he can't stretch the furs to dry, either," Robert added.

"It sounds to me like Dustin is getting the dirty end of this partnership," I said. "He has to run the trapline, then kill and skin the animals all by himself."

Robert looked down at his feet and didn't say anything. Then he raised his head to face me.

"Seely, do we have to tell Mom about it?" he asked. "We could pretend to her that I'm still running traps with Dustin on the days that you are working. That way, she won't worry about me being here alone."

I said that sounded all right to me. I couldn't see why Mom had to know about it. "But on the days you go to the Hollises," I told him, "you'd better be home here before dark, or Mom is going to know about it."

Robert put out his hand to shake on the deal. We wouldn't tell Mom that he wasn't trapping. And he would be home every day before dark. We were shaking hands when Mom walked in the back door.

"Now, what are you two cooking up?" she greeted us.

Robert smiled and said, "Beans and dumplings."

I didn't say anything.

chapter fifteen

*S*eely, I'm of a mind to go to church today," Mom said, as we were eating breakfast. "We can't expect many more days when it will be fit to do."

"But this is the day Arlo Hawks is suppose to be here," I said. "And he might come before we got home."

"Then you'll have to stay here and start dinner," she said.

I didn't especially want to go to church, but it beat staying here at home alone, waiting for a strange boy. And that is what I told Mom.

"Don't argue with me, Seely," Mom said. "I'll have

Dustin and Deidre come on home with me, so make plenty for everyone."

Other than the stewed chicken and raisin pies, I didn't know what to fix for dinner. And Mom hadn't said what to cook. But as soon as she and Robert were out of the house, I started dinner. I put the chicken to stew, and while the raisins were cooking, I made the pie crusts. The pies wouldn't be as good as Mom's pies, but no one would expect them to be.

I wished to heaven that Mom hadn't asked a strange boy to eat with us. He probably wouldn't like a thing we put on the table. I hoped he wouldn't even come. As I fussed around, getting things ready for him, I couldn't believe that a few days ago I was looking forward to having Arlo Hawks here today.

I was glad Dustin and Deidre would be here. I wouldn't have to think of things to say to Arlo Hawks. Deidre was never at a loss for words. She could talk all day and never once repeat herself.

I had my hands in the biscuit dough, when Arlo Hawks got to our house. "And way early," I muttered to myself, as I strewed flour across the room to the door.

Arlo stood stiff and ill at ease on the front stoop, as if, now that he was here, he wasn't sure of his welcome. He looked at the flour on my hands, smiled, and asked, "Am I too early?"

I opened the door wide and returned his smile. "Come on in," I said. "And I'll get the biscuits into the oven."

Arlo Hawks followed me to the kitchen, then stood there looking around.

"Mom and Robert went to church," I said. "They left me at home to cook dinner."

He took off his coat and hung it up. "Can I help you?" he asked.

I pointed a flour-covered hand toward the turquoise pie safe. "The dishes are in there," I said. "You can set the table for six."

When she got home from church, Mom didn't seem the least bit surprised to find Arlo Hawks helping me fix the dinner and get it on the table. Robert and Dustin were openly curious about Arlo, and Deidre seemed more interested in him than I thought was called for. I noticed that she deliberately waited to see where he sat at the table so she could sit next to him.

Mom sat at one end of the table, and Robert at the other end. Deidre sat beside Arlo on one side of the table, and I sat across from her, next to Dustin. Robert and Dustin had their heads together, talking trapping, and the money they expected to make from it. Deidre couldn't take her eyes off Arlo Hawks, as he told her how he was saving his money to go to Detroit in the spring and work on automobiles. Mom and I looked at each other and smiled.

Mom said, "Who wants to return thanks?"

Everyone got quiet. Robert glanced quickly around the table, then he bowed his head. "God is great, God is good, and we thank Him for this food. Amen."

Mom frowned at Robert, but she let it pass.

I think that was the last quiet moment until every bowl and plate on the table had been emptied. The awkward silences that I had feared would happen never happened. It was as if everyone at the table had known each other all their lives.

Finally, Robert said, "Am I the only one who wants a piece of pie?"

Deidre jumped up to help me clear the table, and Arlo Hawks served the pie.

Mom said, "Arlo, sit down. Let the girls do that."

Arlo smiled at Mom. "I'd like to keep in practice," he said. "I may have to wait tables in Detroit while I'm looking for work as an automobile mechanic."

"Are you really going to Detroit?" Deidre asked.

Arlo nodded his head yes. "I'll be there by the first day of May," he replied.

I saw the look that passed between Arlo Hawks and Deidre Hollis, and I knew then, that no matter how good friends we might get to be, Arlo Hawks would never have that look in his eyes for me.

Mom got up from the table, then slid her chair back in place. "You young'uns can clean the kitchen," she said. "I've got mending and patching to do."

Arlo said, "There's no rest for the weary, Mrs. Robinson."

"Nor for pot washers and kitchen scrubbers, neither," Mom retorted.

Then she told Robert to bring in more coal and stir up the fire. "You are going to need all the hot water you can get, to wash these dishes," she said. "Seely can't cook an egg without using every dish in the house."

Mom told me that every day of my life, but I didn't relish having it said in front of company. I started banging pots and pans, and Mom went to her room and closed the door.

When the water was hot, Deidre washed the dishes, Arlo and I dried them, and Robert and Dustin put them away. In no time at all, the kitchen looked as if it had never been used.

Arlo wanted to play gin-rummy or seven-up, now that the table was cleared, but Robert told him that Mom wouldn't allow a deck of cards in the house. "We could play checkers," he said.

But no one wanted to wait turns to play checkers.

Then Deidre suggested that we could all walk downtown. "I want to see where Arlo works," she said.

That seemed like a good idea to Arlo and me, but Dustin and Robert had other things in mind.

"Seely, couldn't Robert go home with me? We need to talk to Grandpa about something."

"He would have to be home before dark."

"I'd have him home before then," Dustin said. "I have to come back and get Deidre."

He and Deidre exchanged a look, then Dustin said, "If anyone should ask, you two girls are still washing dishes."

Dustin and Deidre did the same thing that Robert and I were doing, I thought. They bypassed the truth with their own inventions, when the truth would cause dissension in the house. Knowing this made me feel closer to Dustin and Deidre.

We got our coats and caps and left the house, Robert and Dustin hurrying down the alley toward Bottom Road, and Arlo, Deidre, and I going up the alley to Maple Street.

"I have to be at work at the garage before long," Arlo said. "I won't have time to walk you girls home."

"Oh, we don't mind," Deidre said. "Do we, Seely?"

She didn't wait to find out if I minded or not. She and Arlo Hawks started off and nearly forgot that I was with them until we came to Ray's Garage, where Arlo worked part time.

We didn't stay long at the garage. By the time we got there, it was past time for Arlo to be at work. Deidre and I stood outside the door and talked to Arlo for a few minutes, then he went inside, and we turned back toward home.

We hadn't gone a block, when Deidre complained of being cold. "I didn't notice the cold wind when Arlo was with us," she said.

"It wasn't because Arlo Hawks was shielding you from it," I said. "He's too thin to keep the wind off a bed slat."

"Why, Seely," Deidre said. "How can you say that? It's because he works so hard."

After a few steps, she said, "I can't thank your mom enough for asking Dustin and me to dinner with you all today. I feel like today is the turning point in my whole life."

"Deidre, are you falling for that skinny busboy?"

She turned on me at once. "Don't call Arlo a busboy! He's a mechanic," she said. "And someday, he will have his own garage and be somebody. You just wait and see!"

Deidre ran away and left me to walk alone.

At the end of the next block, Deidre was sitting on the curb waiting for me. I sat down beside her.

"Deidre," I said, "don't be mad. I was only teasing."

She looked at me, then turned her face away.

"I saw the way Arlo Hawks looked at you," I went on. "And I could see he was smitten to the soles of his feet."

This time Deidre didn't turn away. "Do you really think so, Seely?"

I nodded. "Arlo Hawks is not much," I said, "but he is all yours."

"Seely, if we are to stay friends, you'll have to quit talking like that about Arlo."

"Then I won't mention his name," I promised.

We got up and went ahead to my house. Mom was still in her room, and the house was cold as a barn.

"Mom will raise cain when she finds I've let the fire go out," I said, hurrying to put coal in the cookstove.

Deidre reached for the poker beside the heating stove. "You get the fire going in the kitchen," she said. "I'll stir up one in here."

Deidre was a changeable as the weather, I thought. She got mad and yelled at me for teasing her about Arlo, yet she would work like a beaver to build a fire, to keep Mom from getting mad at me.

The coal caught quickly. In no time at all we had fires blazing in both stoves. Later, when Mom came to the kitchen, the whole house was warm and comfortable.

Mom looked around the room. "Where are the boys?"

"Robert went with Dustin to talk to Grandpa Hollis for a while," I said. "They should be home any minute."

I had no more than closed my mouth when there was the scraping of feet on the back steps, and Robert and Dustin walked in the door.

As soon as the boys came in, Deidre got her coat on

125

and said they had to go. "We'll be way after dark getting home," she said.

Mom locked the door behind them, then sagged against it. "I'm glad this day is over," she said. "I couldn't be tireder had I worked all day."

She moved slowly to the table and sat down, cupping her chin on her hands.

I was glad to see the end of this day also. It seemed to me that I had gone to a lot of fuss and bother just so Deidre Hollis could get a boyfriend, while all I got out of it was a long day. Not that I begrudged Deidre the joy she got from Arlo Hawks's company. I'd known before she ever came to the house that Arlo and I had nothing in common except his acquaintance with Mom. We had had nothing else to talk about.

I asked if anyone wanted supper. Robert said he had eaten at the Hollises. "Maybe a piece of pie with a cup of coffee," Mom said. "Then I'm going to bed."

I had pie with Mom, then I cleared away our dishes and went upstairs to my room. Mom called up to me once to remind me that tomorrow was a school day, not to stay up too late. Then she went to bed. The house was quiet a long time before I finally blew out my light and got in bed.

chapter sixteen

The next day was when we had to bring a list of the ingredients for mutton tallow salve to Biology class. As I walked down the hall to the homeroom, I heard someone bemoan the fact that he hadn't been able to find out one thing about the salve. "And very few people who had ever heard of it," he added.

Another one said, "I'll bet Seely Robinson will know what goes into it."

I didn't turn my head or act like I had heard a word. Due to the kindness of Grandpa Hollis, I did know what went into making mutton tallow salve, but I wasn't going to say so until I had to.

Mr. Gibbs called the class to order. "For today's assignment," he said, "we'll start with the first row and follow through. As it comes your turn, read the ingredients you have written on your paper, and we'll discuss how it can be used."

One after another explained that they couldn't find the recipe for making the salve. No one knew anything about it.

"Seely," Mr. Gibbs said, "you tell us what you've found out about the ointment you use on your hands."

I had written the recipe down word for word the way Grandpa Hollis had told it to me, but I had forgotten to ask him how much of each thing to use.

"Besides the mutton tallow," I began.

"Speak up, Seely. The class can't hear you."

I started over again, louder this time. "In the ointment I use, there is mutton tallow, balm of Gilead buds, white pine gum, red precipitate, soap, sugar, and sweet oil. You can use unsalted butter," I added, "if you don't have sweet oil."

"Naturally, she'd know," Arvella Simpson muttered under her breath. "She probably makes her own."

"We are well acquainted with the mutton tallow," Mr. Gibbs said. "But let's see what we can learn of these other things. We'll begin with the balm of Gilead buds."

Ellis Van Waggoner raised his hand. "There's an area called Gilead in ancient Palestine. Could the balm come from there?"

"It doesn't seem likely," Mr. Gibbs replied. "But its source could have originated there."

I leaned in front of Arvella Simpson to speak to Ellis.

"It's a small evergreen tree, Ellis," I whispered. "When its leaves are mashed, you get this yellowish green juice, with a strong odor and a bitter taste."

Ellis raised his hand again and repeated every word I'd told him to the rest of the class. Then he turned to me with a big smile, hands clasped over his head, the sign of a winner.

Mr. Gibbs tried to hide his smile, but it came through in his voice. "Ellis, you and Seely can share that point," he said. Then he asked was anyone familiar with red precipitate.

For a while no one spoke or made any move to do so. Then Hershel Hamm said shyly, "I think that's what my pa once put on my head, when I got lice."

"I believe it can be used in that manner," Mr. Gibbs said. "Precipitate is another name for mercury oxide."

"When I had the pink eye," Virgil Rowe spoke up, "the doctor gave me that to put on my eyes."

Once the other kids started talking, they discovered that they knew something about the salve after all. The stuff I dosed my hands with wasn't such a strange medication as they had thought.

When Mr. Gibbs asked about the white pine gum, I hesitated a moment, then I raised my hand.

"I think the dried inner bark of the tree is boiled down like the sap from a maple tree," I said timidly. "It is used to make cough syrup, too."

That brought on a discussion about cough syrups. It seemed as though everyone in the room had been dosed at one time or another with pine-tar cough medicine, and they all hated it.

When the class was over, Ellis Van Waggoner stopped me as I was leaving the room.

"Seely, do you aim to be a doctor when you get out of school?"

I shook my head no.

"Then how did you know about all that stuff?"

"I know an old gentleman who could have been a doctor," I said, "had he set his mind to it."

Ellis walked to the study hall with me, talking all the while. I listened and nodded my head, but I didn't open my mouth once to answer him.

"I've enjoyed our talk," Ellis said at the door to study hall. "We'll have to do this again sometime."

I said, "Sure, Ellis, anytime at all."

That day marked an end to my days of feeling like an outcast in class. Other than Ellis Van Waggoner, no one was overly friendly, yet they didn't turn up their nose when I walked by either. A few even asked with honest concern about my hands. I stopped hating school. Gradually, I found myself looking forward to the next school day.

Robert went home with Dustin Hollis every afternoon to help Grandpa Hollis scrape and stretch the skins that Dustin brought in from the traps. Deidre walked home with me. On the days when I was going to work somewhere, she would say, "I'll see you later," and walk down Maple Street toward town. Deidre never spoke of Arlo Hawks, and I didn't ask, but I knew she was going to see him at the garage. She was always back at our house when Dustin came home with Robert.

When Mersy Hollis heard that Robert and I would be at home alone on Thanksgiving Day, because Mom had to work, she said that we should come there for dinner. But instead of going to the Hollises, we spent the day cleaning our house and cooking Thanksgiving dinner so it would be ready when Mom got home. We wanted her to know that we had tried to make this a special day, even though she had to work.

It was almost dark at four thirty that day. We had set the table earlier, with the white tablecloth and the good dishes, one place at the end of the table and one on each side. When we saw Mom coming down the alley, Robert hurried to turn on the light over the table, so that she would walk into a bright, cheery room.

Mom came in the back door and stopped when she saw the table. Then without a word, she went straight to her room.

Robert came to where I was standing near the stove, ready to take up the supper. He held his hands over the heat and rubbed them together, as if he was cold. Then he turned to me, and I could see the hurt in his eyes because he thought Mom hadn't noticed our efforts to please her.

"She didn't even see it, Seely."

I wanted to hug Robert, but I settled for a light touch on his shoulder. "She saw everything, little brother," I said. I knew what had happened.

Mom had seen the three places set at a table where once there had been six, and no amount of hopes and prayers and wishful thinking could ever change that memory for her.

"Thanksgiving is just another meal," I told Robert. "I don't know why folks make such a fuss over it."

I bent to take the small roast chicken from the oven. Tears that I didn't know I had fell and sizzled on the hot stove. I brushed impatiently at my face and went on dishing up our supper.

There was little enough to be thankful for this year, I thought. We were running out of groceries, the coal pile was low, and it was three days till Mom would be paid at work.

Robert drew a quick breath, then touched my arm. I turned, and there was Mom, crossing the room in her best dress and Sunday shoes. She had brushed her hair into a loose roll, and it was held in place with her good bone side combs. Not one line showed on her calm face, and her step was as light as spring rain.

"What are you dressed up for?" Robert asked Mom.

Mom smiled and went to take her place at the table. "Robert, I couldn't come to this supper table still wearing my uniform," she said.

Robert sat down beside Mom. He couldn't take his eyes off her. I doubt that he even knew when she took his hand and held it. As I put the hot bread on the table, Mom reached for my hand.

"Sit down, Seely," she said, her brown eyes soft upon me. "Let's be still a moment while we count our blessings."

Still holding our hands, Mom closed her eyes and bowed her head. Robert's eyes met mine across the table, then quickly glanced away.

I looked at Mom's dark auburn hair, the bits of silver shining in the lamplight, the arched brows above the wide-spaced eyes, and the high cheekbones and firm chin. Then I looked at Robert.

I knew his honey-colored hair and blue eyes as well as I knew my own. Even his straight nose, wide-lipped mouth, and firm jaw line were much the same as the ones I saw in the mirror each morning. On Robert, they looked all right. Someday, he might even be handsome, I thought. But what chance in this world had a girl wearing a boy's face? I wished fervently that I had been born with my mother's face, instead of taking after my dad.

I closed my eyes, searching for some blessings that I could count, and in that moment I saw my dad's face as plain as day. The laugh lines around his blue eyes were crinkled up, the way they always were when something amused him, and he seemed to be looking right at me. He shook his head as if to say, "Seely, make the most of what God gave you and stop fighting the things you can't change."

"Seely," Mom said and pressed my hand. "I have thanked God for the children He gave me. And the job so I can provide for you. Would you bless the food so we can eat?"

I am not sure what I said over the dinner that Robert and I had prepared for Thanksgiving. After a quick amen, I opened my eyes. Mom had the strangest look on her face, like she didn't know whether to laugh or to bawl me out.

After supper, when we were doing the dishes, she said, "Seely, your prayers must be getting through to Someone up there. That was one of the best meals I've ever had."

"You were just hungry," I said. "Cornbread and beans

would've tasted good to someone who had worked all day."

Mom looked at me thoughtfully for a moment. "You're right," she said. "They would have."

Mom had the opportunity to eat cornbread and beans many times in the coming weeks. She didn't complain of it. Beans were cheap, and cornbread was filling, and that was the most important thing.

She had discovered that a load of coal would barely last from one payday to the next. After buying coal and paying the rent, Mom had very little money left over to buy groceries. She hadn't paid the light bill for two months. The electric company came and shut off the power soon after Thanksgiving. The money I made doing housework bought kerosene for the lamps.

Robert fussed impatiently at the time it was taking to cure the animal skins. "I'll have money to help out," he said, "as soon as we sell the furs."

chapter seventeen

Grandpa Hollis told the boys that they had prime skins curing, and with the right care, they could make a boodle of money from them. But Robert and Dustin lamented the wait and the long time it took to get the furs ready to sell.

It was little more than a week before Christmas when Grandpa finally told the boys they could take the furs to town.

"Get them to the stores early," he said, "before the other trappers start unloading their furs for Christmas money."

Dustin and Deidre never let on that money was scarce

at the Hollis house, but I figured they were in the same fix we were, and the fur money would come in handy. Dustin was always saying, "When we sell them furs," and then going into a long list of things that he would buy for his mom and grandpa with his share.

The coat and sweater that Dustin wore were nearly threadbare. He needed warmer clothes. I wondered if Mersy Hollis knew about the Salvation Army Store. But I was too shy of courage to mention it to one of the Hollises. They might be the kind who would rather wrap themselves in pride and freeze to death than to wear second-hand clothes.

The boys had stopped trapping for the season. They had brought in the traps from the woods, but the ones along the river were under water so often they hadn't been able to take them up yet.

It seemed like the river was always flooding.

We would get two days of snow, three days of rain, then a two-day freeze. The ice would melt, the ground would thaw, and it would start all over again. White River would rise and overflow the banks, spreading water to the low-lying bottom land and making it impossible for the boys to reach the trapline.

Friday afternoon was one of the freezing times. Robert had gone home with Dustin after school to help take the skins off the stretching boards and pack them in gunnysacks to carry to town the next day. Deidre walked home with me.

I don't know why it should, but the wind seemed colder in the city than it had in the country. We hadn't gone two blocks from school, and I was chilled through and through. I turned the collar of my coat up around my face and ears to keep warm.

"Seely, uncover your face," Deidre said. "I can't make out a word you're saying."

I raised my head. "I said, are you going to town with Dustin to sell the furs?"

"Do you want to go?"

"I'd like to," I said. "I never go anywhere but school, home, and the grocery store."

Deidre kind of laughed. "Then we'll do it," she said. "But don't expect much," she warned me. "We have to go into shack-town looking like tramps and acting like beggars, while we're dickering with the buyers to get a good price for the furs. I've been going with Grandpa and Dustin to sell furs ever since we moved to the farm," Deidre went on. "I was the one who always had to wait on the porch and watch the furs, while Grandpa and Dustin were inside dickering on a price for them. Tomorrow, we'll make the boys take their turn on the porch," she added with a smile.

When we got home, we stirred up the fires in both stoves. Then Deidre helped me carry coal for the night. I told her she didn't need to, but she said that Robert would be doing her share of the chores at the farm. Besides that, she wanted to show me what to wear to shack-town tomorrow, and she couldn't do it until the work was done.

Deidre found an old pair of Robert's overalls that she said were perfect to wear, and a worn flannel shirt that I could wear with them.

"Seely, wear your denim jacket," Deidre said, "and

hide that blond hair under a cap. Where we are going to peddle those skins, you'll be safer if no one knows you're a girl.",

"I've been a girl for nearly seventeen years, and no one has found it out yet," I said, only half-joking.

"They will soon," she answered.

After a while, Deidre started talking about Christmas —the things she would like to do for that day, but had no hopes of doing.

"Are you folks having company for Christmas?"

I shrugged my shoulders. "Not that I know of."

Time was when I would have expected Fanny Phillips and Gus Tyson, but not any more. In the world we lived in now, friends were as scarce as money.

"I thought maybe your mom had invited Arlo Hawks here for dinner," Deidre said.

I shook my head. "I don't know if he is still at the hotel," I said. "Mom never speaks of him."

"Of course Arlo is still at the hotel," Deidre replied. "But with the hotel closing for those two days, he'll have nowhere to go for Christmas dinner."

"Who told you so much about Arlo Hawks?"

Deidre seemed uneasy at my question. I thought I had made her mad again, and she wasn't going to answer me.

"Seely, he told me himself," Deidre said. "I see him a lot. On the days when I'm supposed to walk home with you, but you have to work someplace, I go downtown and talk to Arlo at the garage. We don't go anywhere, or do anything, we just talk. Arlo doesn't want to spend a cent, and I wouldn't let him spend money if he wanted to. We figure by spring, he'll have enough saved to go to Detroit, like he has his heart set on doing."

"You must care an awful lot for Arlo Hawks," I said.

Deidre smiled, and her eyes lit up bright as stars on a clear night. "Seely, it's a different feeling that I have for Arlo. I think about him all the time."

Her face bore testimony to the truth of her feeling for Arlo Hawks. I had an idea that when Arlo went to Detroit, he wouldn't be leaving here alone.

Bright and early Saturday morning, Dustin and Deidre appeared at our back door, looking for all the world like a couple of ragpickers in their patched overalls, the gunnysacks full of furs thrown over their shoulders.

"I thought we'd try Mike Grecco's place," Dustin said. "I hear he's paying top dollar for prime fur. And Grandpa says these are as prime as they come."

I was ready to go, but I couldn't keep my hair up under the cap. Deidre twisted it like a rope and pinned the ends on top of my head. Then she pulled the stocking cap down tight over my ears.

Dustin grinned at the sight of Robert and me in our caps and knitted scarfs. "You look like a pair of book ends," he said.

Every other store in shack-town had a sign in the window saying that furs were bought there. Dustin said we should try them all, then sell the furs to the highest bidder.

We climbed the rickety steps to the wooden porch of the first sign-covered clapboard building. The porch squeaked and the door stuck when we tried to open it.

Dustin said one of us should always stay with the furs, while the others went inside with him while he bargained. And to be fair about it, we'd take turns out front with the gunnysacks. It was to be my turn first.

Fair or not, I was sure that I would freeze to death before the others came back outside. I kept moving around to keep warm, and the porch boards moved as I did, jiggling the gunnysacks until they appeared to hold live creatures. One man came up to me and said, "What have you got in them sacks, boy?"

"Snakes," I said. "Do you want to see them?" I bent over a gunnysack like I was going to untie it, and he left. No one else bothered me.

Dustin, Robert, and Deidre came out of the shack and motioned toward the one at the end of the dirt walk. Robert picked up one sack, and Dustin took the other. Deidre and I followed them single file along the path. "I feel like an Indian squaw," Deidre whispered.

We were in and out of every store in shack-town. Then we took the furs back to Mike Grecco's store to sell them. His prices were still the highest. Mike handed Dustin forty-five dollars and the boys gave him the gunnysacks. That looked like a lot of money until I remembered it had to be split three ways. Then it didn't seem like much, considering how many weeks they'd had to work for it.

On the way home Dustin asked Robert to go with him to take the traps in from the river. Robert got a sick look on his face and turned away.

"There won't be anything in the traps," Dustin said, as if he hadn't noticed Robert's reaction. "I tripped the springs and threw them, the last time I ran the trapline."

"I guess I could do that," Robert replied. "There's no way I could ruin the clothes I've got on today."

We were nearer to the gravel road and the shortcut to the Hollises than we were to our street, and Dustin was in a hurry to get the money home to his grandpa. We cut across vacant lots and alleyways to the gravel road, and then we took the trail down the hill to the Hollis house.

Dustin went at once to his grandpa and put the wad of bills in the old man's hand. "Forty-five dollars, Grandpa," he said. "That's pretty good, isn't it?"

Grandpa Hollis counted out two shares of the money, then he pocketed the bills he'd held in his hand.

"Son, I couldn't have done better," Grandpa said, "had I been doing the dickering myself."

Dustin smiled and reached for the money. Then his expression changed to one of confusion. "Grandpa, this isn't right," he said. "We figured fifteen dollars a piece."

"And I figured you each had an extra five coming to you, for toting them sacks to town," Grandpa Hollis said.

Robert thanked Mr. Hollis, but he didn't touch the money. He stood and stared at that twenty dollars like it was all the money in the world—and he couldn't believe it belonged to him.

"Well," Grandpa said, "what are you boys figuring to do now?"

I think he meant what were they going to do with their money, but Dustin answered with the thought foremost in his mind.

"We're bringing the traps in from the river, Grandpa. We don't plan to do anymore trapping this season."

Dustin went toward the outside door. "Come on, Robert. Let's get it done."

141

Robert picked up his money and handed it to me. Then he followed Dustin out of the house.

I put the money in my overall pocket, and a few minutes later I went home. We had left all the chores undone to go to town with Dustin and Deidre this morning, and there was a lot to do before Mom got home from work tonight.

I didn't bother to change my clothes when I got home. The overalls were more fitted for the purpose of building fires and filling the coal bins than a dress. I could bathe and get into something else after the work was done.

I was still in the overalls when Elvira Spragg knocked at the front door.

"I can't stay," she said, when I asked her in. "This box came in the mail for your mother, and I brought it down."

As I took the box from her hands, I saw that it was from Julie. "Oh, thank you," I said. "Mom will be so happy."

Mrs. Spragg waved her hand as if it was nothing and went back toward home.

I held the box up to my ear and shook it. I ran my hands over the front and sides of the box and held it to me. It wasn't so much what was in the box, but that Julie had remembered and sent us something. Finally, I put the box on the stand table and went on with my work. But I still touched the box every time I walked by it.

I'd had my bath, and supper was on the stove, when Robert and Dustin came to the house. They were wet up to their waists and chilled to the bone. I opened the oven door to let the heat into the room, and they stood there while I got dry clothes for them.

142

I gave Dustin the overalls that I had worn earlier. Then I held a blanket to shield the boys, while they got out of their wet clothes and rubbed themselves dry.

While their pants and shoes were drying in front of the open oven door, Robert and Dustin sat with a blanket wrapped around them and ate potato soup and corn fritters. Robert couldn't seem to stop shivering, even though he was warm and dry.

"You must have gone wading in White River," I scolded.

"We didn't aim to," Dustin said. "Robert slipped and fell in the river, and I jumped in to get him out."

A sudden chill shook me, and I rubbed my arms to wipe away the goosebumps. Our brother Jamie had drowned when he'd been about Robert's age now. And had Dustin not been with Robert today, the same thing could've happened to Robert.

I hugged my arms across my chest to stop their chilling and looked at Robert.

"You are never to go near that river again," I said. "Do you hear me? Not ever again!"

Robert's eyes got wide, and he stopped eating. But he didn't say anything.

"All Mom needs now is to come home and hear that you've been"—I couldn't say drowned—"washed away down White River," I finished.

"Don't yell at him, Seely," Dustin said. "He was in no danger. I was looking after him."

"Dustin," I said, calmer now. "Flooded rivers are always dangerous. Even to a man like you."

"Seely," Robert said quietly, "do we have to tell Mom I fell in the river? She will be mad at me for a week."

143

"We'll not tell her," I said, "unless she asks about your wet clothes. But I think, when Mom sees the money you made from the furs, she will be so happy she won't even see the clothes drying, much less ask about them."

chapter eighteen

Mom spread the twenty
dollars from the furs on the table, and began to earmark
each bill for the things it would buy or pay on the wood
and electricity that we had already used.

"This will get you kids a new pair of shoes," she said,
"and put something on the table for Christmas dinner.
Not to mention another load of coal to keep us warm."

As Mom folded the bills and put them away, the look
of love that she gave Robert would have kept anyone
warm for a long time.

Dustin had left earlier, wearing his damp overalls over
the old ones I had loaned him. Robert's wet things were

hanging on the line behind the stove to dry. The lamp-light didn't reach that dark corner, so Mom hadn't seen them. And we didn't bring it to her attention.

Mom was surprised and happy to see the box from Julie. She touched it and ran her hands over the wrapping, much the same as I had, before she opened it. There was an open letter from Julie on top of the packages in the box. Mom read it aloud, sharing it with Robert and me, then she gave us the gifts that Julie had sent. We couldn't wait till Christmas to open them.

Robert got dominoes and knee-high wool socks from Julie, and I got tan knit gloves. Mom looked at our gifts, and she remarked on how thoughtful it had been of Julie to send us something useful.

Then Mom opened her package. She glanced at the tissue-covered contents and quickly closed the lid. "I've no use for this sort of thing," she said. She picked up the box and went to her room.

I'd had a glimpse inside the box. It looked to me like a silk nightgown.

Robert tried on the knee socks. I put on my knit gloves. They fit fine.

"Now that you've got gloves to wear," Mom said, as she came back to the kitchen, "maybe your hands will heal and stay well."

"I'd give up the gloves and have sore hands, if Julie could be here for Christmas."

Mom came to stand behind my chair and put her hands on my shoulders. "There's no reason why Julie couldn't come home," she said, "had she wanted to see us. You heard me read her letter. She is well, and she's doing fine.

Why, the money she spent on that stuff for me would have paid for her trip here and back."

I thought of the letters that I wrote to Julie, and how I always made things sound better than they were. And I knew as well as if she had told me so herself that Julie was doing the same thing in her letters.

I shrugged Mom's hands away and got to my feet. "I don't believe that," I said. "We don't know what Julie had to give up and do without, so she could send us these things."

Robert said, "Why would she do that?"

"Because she cares about us," I said. "And she wants us to know it."

I took my gloves and went to the loft room. I lit the lamp, then I got out my diary. All the things that I couldn't tell Mom—about the way I felt and what I thought—I wrote down in the little book Julie had given me long ago. "As soon as Robert doesn't need me here," I wrote, "I shall go to live with Julie."

The next morning, a cold, hard rain whipped against the house, discouraging any thought of going to church. Or even getting out of bed, I thought, when I heard Mom call my name. I was glad there'd be no school on Monday. Christmas vacation had begun on Friday and would last until after the new year. I looked at the gray, rain-swept windows and scooted farther under the covers.

"Seely," Mom called from the foot of the stairs. "Do I have to come up there to get you out of bed?"

"I'm up!" I answered, and threw back the covers.

"I can't see the big hurry," I grumbled, as I got dressed

and moved down the steps to the kitchen. "This is no fit day to do anything."

"Speak up, Seely. I can't hear you."

"I didn't say anything," I mumbled.

Mom poured a cup of coffee for herself and hot cocoa for me. "Sit down, Seely. I want to talk to you, while Robert is still asleep."

I figured that she had found Robert's wet clothes, and I was supposed to explain what happened. But it was Julie that Mom had on her mind this morning.

"I've given some thought to what you said about Julie having to sacrifice to give us these gifts," Mom said, "and you may be right. I had in mind to send her a nice card, but in light of this it hardly seems enough."

"You've got time to send Julie a present," I said. "Christmas is still a week away."

"I wondered what you'd say." Mom got up from the table and touched my arm. "Come in here, Seely. I want to show you something."

She went to her room. I thought she was going to show me what Julie had sent her. But Mom went straight to the old round-topped trunk, where she kept all her treasures, and raised the lid.

"I've been making this skirt and blouse for you," she said, taking the things out of the trunk. "And this shirt for Robert. Seely, since you've got two things here to Robert's one, would you like to send the blouse to Julie?"

The blouse she spoke of was a soft, dark brown cotton, with flecks of red and burnt orange, like tiny autumn leaves and bittersweet berries, woven through it. The buttons were clear as water and picked up the colors in the material.

I took the blouse to feel the soft fabric. Tiny stitches, barely visible, held the cuffs on the long sleeves and the round collar. And the buttonholes up the front of the blouse were near to perfect.

"It's a beautiful blouse," I said, and placed it next to the dark brown skirt. It matched exactly.

"There's work yet to be done on that skirt," Mom said.

I smiled at her. "Then we'll send the blouse to Julie," I said. "And I'll keep the skirt."

Now that it was settled, Mom began to have doubts about the blouse. She smoothed a seam and fussed with the collar.

"You don't think she'll mind that it's homemade?" she said. "Or think it old-fashioned?"

"Julie will like it fine," I assured her. "She will be proud to wear it. Anybody would be," I added honestly.

Mom got the box that had held her gift from Julie and folded the blouse to fit in the tissue paper inside it. Then she put the unfinished skirt and shirt back into the trunk and closed the lid.

"I'll wrap and tie this box today," Mom said. "Then tomorrow you and Robert can take it to the post office and mail it. Pick out a pretty card too," she added, "and sign all our names to it."

But Robert and I didn't mail the box the next day, or the day after that either. Robert came down with a cold, and he wasn't able to get out of bed.

I brought in the coal and kept the fires going. Mom

made onion soup for supper. It would be good for Robert's cold. Every time he coughed, Mom gave him a spoonful of onion juice and honey. Robert liked the concoction, but I don't think it helped his cold. By bedtime, he was coughing more than he had all day.

Before she went to bed, Mom asked me to rub mutton tallow salve on Robert's back and chest to loosen his cough.

"I can't put my hands in the stuff," Mom said. "It would smell up the dough at work tomorrow."

I said that I didn't mind. I had to dose my hands with it anyway. I had visions of going back to school after the holidays with my hands soft and white. If mutton tallow would do that for me, I couldn't complain of its odor.

Before I went to bed, I banked the fires and put a hot flat iron at Robert's feet to keep him warm. But he must have slept cold anyway. I heard him coughing all night long.

Robert was sick for three days. Every morning Mrs. Spragg came down and stayed with him while I went to her house to clean and empty trash baskets. Then, in the afternoon, Dustin and Grandpa Hollis would come to see Robert. Dustin would fill the coal boxes while he was there, and Grandpa Hollis entertained Robert with his stories of the olden days.

Mom fussed over him at night, wondering aloud where he could have caught such a cold. Robert conveniently fell asleep at this point and avoided having to explain.

I didn't have to work for Mrs. Spragg the day that Robert got up for the first time. Elvira Spragg didn't come that morning. Robert stayed up till noon, and then went back to bed.

He was sleeping when Dustin and Deidre came by on their way to do their Christmas shopping. Dustin offered to stay with Robert and keep him company while I went to town with Deidre.

"Dustin, are you sure you don't want to go?" I asked.

"I'd rather stay here," he said. "I was only going so Deidre wouldn't have to go alone."

"Then I'll go," I said. "We have a package to mail, and I want to get something for Mom, and—"

"Tell me on the way, Seely." Deidre laughed and handed me my coat.

We went to the post office first, to mail the package to Julie and get it off my hands. Then we went shopping in every store around the courthouse square. I had the dollar Mrs. Spragg had paid me for my work this week and the change left over from the parcel postage, but I didn't spend a penny until we went into the five and dime store.

I bought Mom a box of handkerchiefs and chose two five-cent Christmas cards. One was for Julie, and the other one was for Robert. I saw many things I'd have liked to give Robert, but even if I had the money, I wouldn't have dared. He couldn't give me anything, and it would have shamed him to get gifts and not be able to give one. Deidre got perfume for her mother and brown cotton socks for Grandpa Hollis.

Deidre said that she was done with her trading, we could start home whenever I was finished with mine. She hadn't bought anything for Dustin.

"What are you giving Dustin for Christmas?" I asked.

"I made hickory nut fudge for Dustin," she said. "He gave me this money for a present, and he'd be hurt if I spent any of it on him."

151

chapter nineteen

*T*he snow began on Christmas Eve, blowing and slithering down the alley and across our yard like a living thing, hurrying on its way to somewhere else. And I hoped it would keep going until it got there. We didn't need more snow and cold, not with the coal pile so low that it was hard to find a good-sized lump to put in the stove. I filled the bucket with the biggest lumps I could find and took it inside.

"We're going to have a white Christmas," Robert said, gazing out the kitchen window at the snow.

"Only till the coal dust settles on it," I said, dumping my load of coal into the box.

152

"What do you think we'll get for Christmas, Seely?"

Robert was still feeling puny from the cold he'd had earlier in the week, and I humored him. When he had asked the same question this morning, I had made a game of it, naming off all the things a boy his age would want to get, and the ones I had no hopes of ever getting. But I didn't want to play now.

"You will have to wait until morning to find out," I told him.

I knew what we were getting—if Mom had got her sewing done. But I would let it be a surprise to Robert.

When Mom came in from work, she stamped the snow off her feet and said it was getting deeper by the minute.

"It wouldn't surprise me," she said, "to find we are snowed in here come morning."

We weren't snowed in the next morning, but we might as well have been. It was so cold and blowing that we didn't want to go out.

Mom made thin apple pancakes for breakfast, with scorched sugar syrup and long, crisp strips of bacon.

"Come and eat," she said. "Then I've got something for you."

Robert could hardly wait until the table was cleared to see what he was getting for Christmas. To hurry Mom along with her giving, he brought our tissue-wrapped gift to the table and gave it to her. Mom waited until we had our presents from her, then she unwrapped her gift.

She rubbed the soft handkerchiefs between her fingers and thumb. "I never feel dressed up," she said, "until I have a nice hanky in my pocket."

As soon as I opened my present, I knew that Mom had been to the Salvation Army Store again. It seemed like ever since she had discovered that place the only things brought into the house that weren't used and second-hand were the groceries we put on the table.

Folded on top of the brown wool skirt that Mom had made for me was a soft green cardigan sweater. It looked almost new, but there was a button missing at the neckline.

"The woman at the store told me that the girls never use that top button," Mom said. "The sweater is worn over a blouse, and they don't button it all the way."

"It's beautiful," I said, holding the sweater against my chest. "Look how well it goes with my complexion."

Mom didn't even glance my way. "Don't be vain, Seely," she said. "I didn't get that sweater to show off your fairness. It's to keep you warm."

I folded the sweater and put it away.

Along with the shirt, Robert got a blue sleeveless sweater from the Salvation Army Store. It had a vee neckline and brightly colored diamond-shaped figures on the front. The back of the sweater was plain blue. Mom smiled at the pleased look on Robert's face.

"I hope it fits you," she said.

Robert slipped the sweater on over his pajama top and said it couldn't fit better. "Not even if you'd made it yourself," he told Mom.

The three of us sat and talked of the presents this day had brought us. No one seemed willing to speak of what the year had taken away. Family, friends, a feeling of belonging somewhere; they were all gone.

154

We talked, but none of us said what was really on our minds.

The hotel was closed the day after Christmas. Mom was at home with us all day. Around noontime a big truck went down our alley, pushing the snow into our driveway as it cleared the way to Bottom Road and on toward the Hollises.

Mom said thank goodness the alley was cleared, now if she could just get to it. Robert and I took that as a hint to make a path for her through the snow, and we went outside to shovel the snow away from our door.

Robert looked longingly toward Bottom Road and wondered aloud what Dustin and Grandpa Hollis were doing, now that the trapping was done.

"Maybe he and Deidre will come to see us later," I said. "They know we'll want to stay here on Mom's day off."

Robert watched and waited, but Dustin didn't come.

We had no more than finished eating our supper that evening when Elvira Spragg knocked on the kitchen door and walked in.

"I just got the word that old Dun Hollis was found dead in his bed this morning," she said. "They are sitting up with him tonight, and he's to be buried tomorrow. I thought you would want to sit up with Mersy and me," she added, "seeing as how the young'uns are such good friends."

Mom looked at Robert and me, then she turned to Elvira Spragg. "I don't like to leave the children alone at night," she said uneasily, torn between her duty as a neighbor and her responsibility as a mother.

"We'll be all right," I said. "There's nothing here in the dark that is not here in the daylight."

Mom hesitated a moment longer, then she went to get her coat and hat.

I locked the door behind Mom, then Robert and I cleared the table and did the dishes. Robert hardly said a word while we were busy neatening up the kitchen, but when I started to the loft room, he wanted to talk.

"Seely, did we ever have a grandpa, like Grandpa Hollis?"

"No," I said, "they all died before we were born."

"What did they die of?"

"I don't know," I said. "The flu, I guess, and different things."

"Winter is hard on the old people, ain't it, Seely?"

"Robert, I don't think the cold winter had anything to do with Grandpa Hollis dying. Probably, his heart just quit working."

He didn't say anything else right then, but later, when we were banking the fire for the night, Robert said, "I don't care what Mom says, I'm going to the funeral tomorrow. I'll go to the Hollises early, then Dustin and I can go together."

Mom took the day off and we all went to the funeral. And we stayed to see the first frozen chunks of earth dropped into the open grave. Standing in the churchyard with Deidre, I couldn't help thinking of the day Grandpa Hollis had told Mom that the Loon Creek Christian Church was the last place on earth he ever wanted to go. And now it was.

Elvira Spragg walked home with us from the funeral.

She said she had never seen such a turnout for a winter burying. "But then," she said, "Dun Hollis was well thought of in these parts."

I knew there were four young people who thought a lot of Grandpa Hollis, and we were walking right behind Mom and Mrs. Spragg.

"I know everyone thought Mom and Grandpa hated each other," Deidre said, "but that isn't so. Mom told me herself that Grandpa saved her sanity. She said if it hadn't been for his nagging and pushing her, after Dad left us, she would have sat there and died. But Grandpa got her fighting mad and she came out of it."

"And they've been at it ever since," Dustin said. Then, musingly, he added, "I wonder who she will fight with now that he's gone?"

Deidre made a face and replied, "Who do you think?"

The car that had brought Mersy Hollis home from the funeral was sitting in front of the house. We didn't go in. After Mom and Mrs. Spragg had said again how sorry they were about Mr. Hollis, we went on home.

Robert went with Elvira Spragg. "To check the furnace, and see that the house is warm," he said, leaving Mom and me to build up the fires at our house.

"What has gotten into that boy?" Mom said.

"He blames the cold for Grandpa Hollis passing away," I said. "He's afraid it will take Mrs. Spragg the same way."

Mom smiled and kind of shook her head. "I wonder where he ever got a notion like that," she said.

I could have told her where I thought Robert had got the notion, but it would've upset her. Since she hadn't mentioned that it was a bitterly cold day like this one when we had buried Dad, I couldn't be the one to bring it up.

Robert and I had intended to go to the Hollises the next day as soon as our work was done. But at midmorning it began to snow again and blow up a storm. We couldn't leave the house. We didn't see Dustin and Deidre until we went back to school on Monday.

chapter twenty

When I got out of school Monday afternoon, Deidre had already gone. I turned my coat collar up around my face and hurried along to the elementary school. Dustin and Robert were waiting inside the door, but there was no sign of Deidre.

I said that I supposed Deidre had chores to do at home, and she'd taken the shortcut. Dustin didn't say one way or the other. He walked home with Robert and me and stayed to help us with our chores.

It was getting dusk when Deidre came hurrying into the house all out of breath. "I had to go downtown," she said. "I didn't aim to be so long."

Dustin got into his coat and cap and started to the door. "We'd best not tarry, Deidre. Mom will be coming after us."

Deidre hesitated for a moment, then she turned and followed Dustin out the door. They were both running as soon as they cleared the kitchen steps.

No more than a minute later, Mom got home from work. She was breathless too, but we soon learned it wasn't from hurrying.

"I've had my pay envelope stolen," Mom said, her voice trembling. "My coat was in the cloakroom and I had the envelope pinned to my coat pocket, but someone ripped it loose and took it."

Mom still wore her coat. She turned the pockets out to show us they were empty. "What kind of a person steals the last cent a body has?"

Robert stared at Mom. He seemed unable to grasp what she was telling us. I backed to a chair and sat down. Chills ran over me like someone stepping on my grave, and I shivered. I knew what it meant to Mom to have her two-week's pay stolen, and I was scared. I could see no way on earth that we could get by for two more weeks without that money.

There was just the slag and coal dust left in the shed. The last of the coal was in the bin beside the stove. Mom had ordered coal two days after Christmas, but the man at the coalyard had told her it had to be paid for in advance. We wouldn't get it now.

"Whoever took it had to know I needed that money to live on," Mom said. "I wouldn't be there if I didn't need the money."

Mom was so filled with indignation that I don't think she even realized she was crying.

I got up and poured her a cup of coffee. Robert took her hand and coaxed her to the table. After a few sips of hot coffee, Mom said, "Spilt milk and strayed horses." She mopped at her face with her hand. "Why do we always cry and moan the loudest over the things we can't change?"

"Maybe that's why," Robert said. "If we could change things, we'd do it. We wouldn't sit and cry about it."

Mom put out her hand to touch Robert and draw him closer.

"What have I brought you kids to?" she said.

Mom sat quietly for a moment, turning the wide gold wedding band round and round on her finger. She sighed wearily.

"Your daddy thought he was doing the right thing when he moved us all to Greene County," she said quietly. "I thought I was moving for the better when I brought you here. Your daddy and me, we were both wrong. We should have stayed on the farm and waited out this depression. But, to our sorrow, we had to find it out the hard way."

Mom pushed herself to her feet, like she was tired to death. "Put supper on the table, Seely, while I wash my face. Maybe things won't look so black after we've had a good meal."

Robert set the table while I took up supper. I looked at the plain fare and wished aloud that I had something special to put on the table, just this once.

"We could open a jar of those tomato preserves that

Mrs. Spragg gave me," Robert said. "That would go good with the meatloaf, and Mom would like it."

That's what we did. And Mom liked it.

After supper, Mom brought out the tea tin that held my earnings and a small leather coin purse. She emptied the change from the tea tin, then she took a few bills from the coin purse and smoothed them flat on the table before us.

"Right there is every cent we have in the world," Mom said. "And it has to last until the fifteenth of the month."

Robert was stacking the change according to its worth and counting it as he went along. "Whew," he said. "That's not much money."

"No, it's not," Mom replied. "It won't pay the rent, nor buy a ton of coal. But I wanted you to know how much we had on hand and what to expect from it."

She looked from Robert to me, then she added, "It's your earnings, Seely. And what is left from Robert's fur money. You kids say how it is to be spent."

I looked at the money. Mom was right. It wouldn't buy a ton of coal, or pay the rent. But it would pay the water bill, buy groceries, and keep us in firewood. The main things were food and heat and water, I told Mom— after we came to an understanding with Mrs. Spragg about the rent.

"Mrs. Spragg won't say a word when she hears why you can't pay her," I said. "I know we can get firewood from the Hollises, at least for a little while. Robert can help Dustin cut the wood, then haul it here on the sled."

Mom's face lost its tautness, and a slow look of under- standing took its place. "I've been nearly out of my mind," she said, "wondering what to do. But the way you tell it, Seely, we've no cause to worry for a while yet."

"You'd have seen that for yourself," I said, "given time for the shock to wear off. You can talk to Mrs. Spragg, and I'll ask Dustin about the firewood. We'll know then whether it's time to worry or not."

Mom got up and went to the front window and looked out toward the Spragg house. "Her lights are on up there," she said. "I'll go talk to Elvira now and get it off my mind."

It seemed like no time at all before Mom was back home again, looking more worried than she had when she left. I was almost afraid to ask, but I had to know.

"What did Mrs. Spragg say about the rent?"

"She wasn't there," Mom said, moving to warm herself at the stove. "I spoke to her nephew, Sam Prophet."

Mom turned to face me, and I thought she looked frightened, as well as concerned. "Elvira Spragg is in the hospital with a broken hip," she said. "Sam Prophet and his wife are moving into her house. He said he'd be taking care of his aunt and her affairs from now on. I could pay my rent to him."

"I don't like the man," Mom said fervently. "And I'll not ask him to extend my rent. After work tomorrow, I will go to the hospital and speak to Elvira about it."

With that, Mom smacked her hands together and worked one against the other, as if she was dusting this day's misfortune away like excess flour after the biscuits were made.

"We'd better get to bed, Seely. Morning will be on us, and we won't be ready for it."

Mom waited till I called down from the loft room,

then she blew out the light on the kitchen table and went to her room.

The loft room was cold. It seemed to take forever for my bed to get warm. I curled into a ball in the middle of the bed and thought of other things to keep my mind off my cold feet.

I thought of the money I could have made this week, if Mrs. Spragg hadn't broken her hip. Then I scolded myself for even thinking such a thing. If Mom hadn't had the electricity turned on in the house when we moved here, and if we'd gone ahead and used the kerosene lamps like we had always done, we wouldn't be in such dire need of money.

And the money she paid out for water in the kitchen, when we had a good pump in the yard, was a wasteful, uncalled-for luxury. If we had wrapped the pump earlier in the year, it wouldn't have frozen solid. We'd have all the water we could use, and it wouldn't cost a cent.

If Mom hadn't been so prideful about the wood Gus Tyson was giving us for free . . . If. If. If. I must have had a string of if's as long as my arm, by the time I got warm and fell asleep.

chapter twenty-one

Dustin and Deidre were
at our house the next morning before Robert and I were
ready for school.

"We came early," Dustin said, "so we'd have time to
get warm." He shivered, and rubbed his hands together
over the cookstove. "I'm ready to head for a warm
climate and stay there forever," he added.

"Don't leave just yet," I said. "We need your help."

Then I went on to tell him about Mom's money being
stolen, and what I had in mind for fuel. "I've allowed
two dollars for firewood," I told him, "and we'll need
wood until the fifteenth when Mom gets paid again."

"You don't need to pay me," Dustin said. "We've got cords of wood in our barn that you can have."

I explained to Dustin that Mom wouldn't hear of taking charity. "The money I'm offering is not nearly enough," I said, "but it will be more than enough to pay your way to the show on Saturday."

"Then we'll take it," Dustin said. He nudged Robert. "Buck Jones is on this week," he added.

Robert and Dustin left for school ahead of Deidre and me. They walked fast to keep warm, and we never did catch up to them. But now and then the sound of their voices drifted back to us.

Deidre told me that she had heard it from Arlo Hawks that Mom's money had been taken. "Arlo didn't work at the hotel yesterday," she said, "but when he went in to get his pay, everyone was talking about it."

"Did Arlo Hawks have any idea who took the money?"

Deidre shook her head. "He didn't say," she replied. "We hadn't seen each other since before Christmas, and we had other things on our minds."

We walked a ways without saying anything. Then I asked, "Does your mother know that you are seeing Arlo Hawks?"

"Nobody knows that I'm seeing Arlo," Deidre said. "Except you and Dustin. And Dustin won't tell."

I slipped my arm through Deidre's. "Neither will I," I promised.

For the rest of the week, Robert went to the Hollises to help Dustin cut wood. Deidre walked home with me. One afternoon, she went to Ray's Garage to see Arlo

Hawks, but she was back at our house when Dustin and Robert got there with the split firewood.

Dustin came to the house about noon on Saturday. The sled was piled high with wood, tied down with rope to hold it in place. Robert helped Dustin unload the sled, then they came inside to get warm.

"Seely, I brought you enough wood to last awhile," Dustin said.

"I see you did," I said and thanked him. "I'll get your money, so you boys can make the first show."

I got the tea tin from Mom's room and counted out fifty cents apiece.

Mom had taken money out of the tin to pay the water bill, but nothing else. I figured if I bought only what we needed to get by, there was enough money to last until Mom got paid.

After the boys left the house, I finished hanging the wet wash to dry on the balcony line. As I was emptying the rinse water into the sink, I heard someone knock at the front door, then try to open the screen door.

I ran to lock the kitchen door, then I went to the front of the house. I had to open the solid wood door to see who was there. A big, red-faced man raised his hand and struck the siding, even after he had seen that I had opened the door.

I said, "What do you want?"

He tried again to open the screen. Then he peered through it, trying to see into the house. "Are you one of the Robinson kids?"

I said that I was.

"Sam Prophet here," he said. Like everyone ought to

know who he was. "I'm looking after Elvira Spragg's property while she's in the hospital."

"Yes," I said. "My mother told me."

He put his hands to his face to shade his eyes and stepped closer to the screen door. I inched the solid door forward, so I could close it quickly, if need be.

"Is your mom at home? I want to look this house over and talk to her about the rent she has been paying."

He reached for the doorknob and stepped to one side, as if he expected me to unlock it and let him in.

"Mom is not here," I said. "And Mrs. Spragg is the only one who has a right to come in here. We pay our rent to her."

I quickly closed the door and locked it. I leaned against the door until my knees stopped knocking, then I went to the front window and looked out. Sam Prophet was gone. But huge footprints made a path in the unbroken snow from our front door to the Spragg place.

Even though I knew that no one could get into the house, I kept looking over my shoulder all afternoon as I went about my work and made supper.

I told Robert and Dustin about Sam Prophet when they came back from the movies. "He wanted to come in and look around," I said. "But I wouldn't let him."

"Are you going to tell Mom he was here?"

"I don't think so," I said. "I can see no sense in getting her riled, when there's nothing she can do about it."

"She's sure to see his tracks in the snow," Robert said.

"When she asks me, I'll say he came for the rent," I said.

Dustin ate supper with Robert and me, then he stayed to talk to Mom awhile after she got home. When he left, he didn't take his sled with him. "I'll get it the next time I see you," he told Robert.

Later that night, I decided I'd better tell Mom that Sam Prophet had been at the house to talk to her about the rent. Mom said, "Humph! That man!" And nothing more was said about it.

We didn't know until Deidre came by for school on Monday morning that Dustin had run away from home. While Mersy Hollis and Deidre were at church on Sunday, Dustin had taken a change of clothes and what was left of the fur money his grandpa had given him and gone away.

"He told Mom that he was going to leave home," Deidre said. "But she didn't believe him."

I couldn't believe it either. Yet Dustin had told Robert way last fall that he wouldn't stay at home, if it wasn't for Grandpa Hollis. And now Grandpa Hollis was gone, so Dustin felt there was nothing to keep him there any longer.

At first, Robert walked alone, a little ahead of Deidre and me. Then he stopped and waited to walk the rest of the way to school with us. At the elementary school, Deidre said, "Robert, would you go to Dustin's room and get his things out of his desk?"

Robert turned his face to Deidre. "He might come back."

"No, Robert. He won't come back," Deidre said softly. "He would've gone long ago, but he couldn't bear to leave Grandpa."

Robert nodded his head. "I'll get his things," he said, "and take them to your mother after school."

We went on toward the high school. Robert looked

169

after us for a moment, then he turned and went into the schoolhouse.

Three days later, Mom and I were awakened in the middle of the night to be told that Robert had tried to run away from home.

chapter twenty-two

*E*ither the unusual sound of a car stopping in the driveway woke me, or else it was the men's voices speaking outside the kitchen door. But I was wide awake when the knocking began.

"Seely," Mom called softly, "come down here."

I was already halfway down the steps to the kitchen when she lit the lamp. "I'm here," I whispered.

Mom had Dad's old shotgun clutched tight in both hands like a club. "You open the door," she said. "But be ready to slam it shut, when I say so."

I opened the door wide enough to see two policemen

and Robert standing on the back steps. Mom saw them too. She dropped the shotgun like it was red hot.

"Robert!" she said. "What are you doing out of bed at this hour?"

Robert ducked between Mom and me and went running toward the front room.

One of the officers said, "It looks like he belongs here." And they turned to leave.

"Not so fast," Mom said. "Where did you find Robert? I thought he was in bed," she added.

"He was walking out northwest of town," the officer told her. "Said he was going to Jubilee to see a friend. But he was near frozen, and he didn't argue when we told him that we were bringing him home."

Mom said, "Thank you for that." And the officer said, "You're welcome." He turned back toward the patrol car, and Mom closed the door and locked it.

For just a moment, she rested against the door. Then she turned and saw me standing there in my nightgown. "For heaven's sake, Seely, go to bed!" She spoke as if I had been the one who had got her out at this hour. As I went upstairs, I wondered what Mom would have to say to Robert for what he had done.

The next morning, when I called Robert to get him up for school, he said he wasn't going. "Just leave me alone," he muttered.

"You've got to go to school," I said. "If you don't go, they will send a truant officer here, and then you'll really be in trouble."

I started to the kitchen to fix our breakfast. Robert still hadn't moved.

"Get out of that bed and get dressed," I called over my

shoulder. "I'm leaving for school as soon as I eat, and you are going with me."

"You can't tell me what to do," he yelled. "You are not my mother!" He was on his feet, and he was angry.

"No, I'm not your mother," I shouted back at him. "But I'm the next best thing! You'll do as I say, or I'll give you the licking of your life!"

We stared angrily at each other. Then Robert started to grin sheepishly. "Only because I'd let you give me a licking," he said. "You're not big enough to do it without my help."

I started to laugh, but it didn't come out that way. I choked back the tears and hurried on to the kitchen. By the time the oatmeal was ready to eat, Robert was dressed and ready for school. I wanted to ask him why he had done such a stupid thing as slipping away during the night. But I couldn't think of a way to ask the question without making him mad again.

The ground was frozen and the snow packed hard under our feet, but the wind that whipped down the street lifted the loose snow and flung it into our faces, bringing tears to our eyes. I told Robert that I was glad we had warm coats this morning, even if they had come to us by way of the Salvation Army Store. We could pull the collars up around our ears and keep a little of the wind out of our faces. He just grunted his reply.

"Something else I'm glad for," I said. "Today is Friday. I won't have to go out of the house tomorrow. Except to go to the toilet," I added.

I knew that Robert wasn't listening to me. He had his face tucked into his coat, and he didn't even look up.

When the elementary school came in sight, Robert

raised his head and turned to me. "Seely, let's walk to Jubilee tomorrow. I want to know why Gus and Aunt Fanny haven't been here to see us."

I didn't want to tell Robert no and start another fight with him. So I kept quiet.

"I was heading for Gus Tyson's last night when the police stopped me," Robert said. "But they wouldn't pay any attention to you and me in the broad daylight. We could be there and back before dark."

What he was suggesting could get us into a mess of trouble, and I told him so. "We'd never make it to Jubilee and back in one day," I said. "And what's more, Mom would have us put away for certified idiots if we tried it."

"Seely, if we went by the old logging road that Gus Tyson used the day he moved us here, we'd be there and back in no time."

I shivered and shoved my hands deeper into my coat pockets.

"But we would freeze to death, Robert."

I should have given him a flat no to begin with and told him to forget it. He had an answer to every argument I could come up with against going to Jubilee.

When we parted at the grade school, Robert skipped down the walk like it was all settled and he couldn't wait for tomorrow to get here.

As soon as Mom closed the door behind her the next morning, Robert called my name. I wondered how long he had been awake, just waiting for Mom to go to work so he could get me up.

"Seely," Robert said from the top of the stairs, "put these things on so you won't get cold." A thick bundle landed on the foot of my bed.

"Hurry it up," he said. "We've got to get started while it is still dark."

I gave a sigh of resignation and got out of bed. Since Robert seemed to be determined to go to Jubilee today, I might as well go with him. When Mom heard of it, it wouldn't matter whether I was with Robert, or here at home. As the oldest, I'd be held to account for it.

I unrolled the bundle that Robert had pitched onto my bed and began to get dressed. Over my own underclothes, I put on a pair of Robert's long underwear, heavy knee socks, and a flannel shirt. Then I buttoned his coveralls to my chin and went downstairs.

chapter twenty-three

*I*t was breaking day as Robert and I left the city of Bedford behind us and headed down the narrow country road that would take us to Jubilee.

As I stumped along beside Robert, I wondered what he hoped to accomplish by talking to Gus Tyson. I thought Mom had made it clear, when she bought that first load of coal, that she didn't want Gus coming to the house or bringing firewood to her from his sawmill.

If Mom wouldn't tell us why she had broken with Gus Tyson, it was a cinch we wouldn't learn anything from him.

"This is a fool's errand," I grumbled. "A wild goose chase that will gain us nothing but frostbite."

Robert didn't seem to notice the grumbling, or else he chose to ignore it. "I can put up with frostbite," he said calmly. "It's having Mom's old friends—and ours—leaving and never saying why that I can't handle. I guess it's the not knowing that gets me," he added.

I realized then why Robert wanted so much to talk to Gus Tyson. He needed someone who would give him the answers to the questions that were bothering him. And Gus would be the one most likely to know, better than Mom or me.

Not long after sunup, an old automobile with isinglass over the windows stopped to give us a ride. We couldn't see the driver until we opened the door to get in the car. Then we saw that it was the Reverend Mister Paully, the preacher from Jubilee.

Mr. Paully said he was on his way home from his night watchman's job in Bedford. He would be pleased to carry us right to Fanny Phillips's door.

"I don't often see Gus Tyson," the preacher said, "what with me working nights and sleeping days. Gus is away on Saturday and Sunday, working on that house he bought in Oolitic."

After a while we started up a long, curvy hill. I recognized the lane that led back to the Tyson house where we used to live. Mr. Paully frowned and motioned toward the lane.

"Gus sold his house back there to a city man, name of Jacob Dove," he said. His mouth puckered like he had bit a lemon. "The man don't aim to live there. Going to use it for hunting and fishing, he told Gus."

I felt like the ground had been cut from under my feet. I had always counted on that place being there, to go back to, if we couldn't make it in the city. Now there was no place left to fall back on.

The Reverend Mister Paully let us out in front of Fanny Phillips's house in Jubilee. "Come and see Nellie," he said. "She gets lonesome to see you young'uns."

Gus Tyson wasn't at home. "In Oolitic, working on that house," Fanny said disapprovingly. But she made Robert and me welcome, helping us out of the heavy clothes we wore and fixing hot sandwiches.

Fanny Phillips poured coffee for all three of us, then she poured milk and sugar in mine and Robert's cups until we couldn't taste the coffee. While we ate, Fanny sat and complained about Gus Tyson. Since he was her brother, she could complain if she wanted to, I thought. But neither Robert nor I spoke a word against him.

She said that since Gus had sold the farm and bought the house in town, he spent more time in Oolitic than he did here at home. "He says he figures to move in there this coming spring," Fanny said.

"Mr. Paully told us that the place where we used to live had been sold," I said. Then I added, "I always liked that house."

Fanny made a snorting sound, "Wait until you've seen this house in town," she said. "It has two bathrooms inside. One for the family and one at the foot of the stairs for the maid."

"A bathroom for the maid?" I had to smile. The idea of Gus hiring a maid, when Fanny Phillips had kept house for him all this time, was something to smile about.

"I'll have to talk to Gus," I said. "After the work I've been doing, I think I could qualify for that job as a maid."

I had spoken in jest, but Fanny Phillips took my words as gospel truth.

"Seely, you mustn't say anything to my brother about the house," she said seriously. "He wouldn't like to hear that I had been talking about him behind his back."

She got to her feet and switched the subject to Robert and me and the reason for our visit. I stammered something about Robert wanting to talk to Gus, but since he wasn't here, we'd have to be starting back to Bedford.

"I'll just trim Robert's hair for him, while he's here," Fanny said. "Then I'll drive you home."

Fanny Phillips questioned Robert as she clipped and trimmed his hair. He side-stepped every other question with one of his own. I listened with amazement as Robert bypassed one personal inquiry after another, never telling Fanny anything that he considered of no concern to her.

On the way home in Fanny's car, I wondered how he did it. Any time that I had ever tried to evade a question, or suppress an answer, I would get tongue-tied, stutter, and turn red in the face. Yet Robert had remained calm and collected, as if it came natural to him to parry words with Fanny Phillips.

But even so, before we got home, Fanny got the best of Robert. She found out from him that Mom didn't know we had come to Jubilee, and he wasn't eager for her to know it.

"Well," Fanny said, when she was dropping us off at home, "I won't be seeing your mom for a while. So it is up to you to explain how Robert got a haircut today."

179

I smiled at Fanny's slyness. "We'll tell Mom as soon as she gets home from work," I said. "She will be glad to have some word of you."

"I figured you would," she said. "I'll tell Gus that you were looking for him." She waved and drove away.

Robert run his hand over his clipped head and watched as Fanny Phillips turned from our alley. "Son of a gun," he said, "She tricked me!"

We stopped at the woodpile on our way inside to fill our arms with firewood. There were maybe three good armloads left in the shed.

"We'll be out of wood by tomorrow night," Robert said. "When I get the fire built in the cookstove, I'll take the sled and go to the Hollises for another load of wood."

"Wait until morning," I told Robert, "and I'll go with you."

"You'll get bawled out for going with me today," he said, "and it was all for nothing."

Robert sounded so discouraged that I didn't have the heart to say I'd told him so, that we never should have considered going to Jubilee. Instead, I tried to cheer him.

"It wasn't for nothing, little brother," I said. "You got a haircut, and we found out why we haven't seen Gus Tyson lately."

"That won't carry much weight with Mom," he said. "We would be better off to not even mention Gus to her."

As soon as the fire in the cookstove had taken the chill off the room, we got out of our heavy wraps and into our everyday clothing to do the housework and make our supper.

Usually, this was the day Mom worked late. But this evening, she came home no more than an hour later than a regular work day.

"I'll have to go in tomorrow, because I didn't work late tonight," Mom said. "But it can't be helped. The things I had to do after work today couldn't be put off any longer."

We were eating supper when the coal truck came and dumped a ton of coal in the lean-to shed. Mom turned toward the sound of the lump coal striking the shed floor and nodded her head.

"We'll be all right now," she said. "I went to see Mrs. Spragg and finally paid the rent I've been owing her. She's going to be there quite a while. Old bones mend slowly." Then Mom added, "Monday, I'll get the groceries. You kids can come to the hotel after school and help me carry things home."

Robert had been quiet, not wanting to draw attention to himself, but now he said, "What if somene steals the grocery money while you're at work?"

Mom patted her bosom. "Nobody's getting their hands on this money," she said.

Mom went to her room. Then, after a while, she called to say we should bank the fire and lock the doors. She was going to bed. Robert seemed to take the first full breath of air since Mom had gotten home.

chapter twenty-four

*R*obert and I did everything on Sunday that we had skipped doing the day before when we had gone to Jubilee. The minute Mom was out of the house, I started heating the water to do the washing. While I made the beds and swept the floor, Robert carried in coal and filled the bins beside both stoves. We didn't stop for a moment until the laundry was done and the clothes were drying on the balcony wire line. Then I made pancakes and applesauce, and we sat down to eat.

"We were sure lucky last night," Robert said. "Mom didn't even ask what we'd been doing all day."

"She had other things on her mind last night," I reminded him. "But when she gets home today, we'd better tell her."

But we didn't get the chance to tell her we had gone to Jubilee. She knew it before she ever stepped foot into the house.

I was setting the table for supper when I heard a car stop outside the door. A moment later, Mom came in with Gus Tyson.

"Gus came by as I was leaving the hotel," Mom said. "He brought me home."

"I was coming this way." Gus smiled at Robert. "Fanny said you wanted to talk to me."

Robert looked like he would be happy if the floor opened up and swallowed him. And I would've gladly gone with him. The one thing I didn't need was a bawling out from Mom in front of Gus Tyson.

Mom said, "Seely, set another place at the table. Gus is staying to supper with us."

I went to do her bidding.

When I'd started supper, I had told Robert that I was going to cook everything in one pot. That way, there wouldn't be so many pans to wash afterwards. I stewed the chicken until the meat fell from the bones, then I added potatoes, carrots, and onions and let them simmer in the meat broth. Just before time for Mom to get home, I had made biscuits, put them over the stew, then put it all in the oven to bake.

Now as I dished up the concoction I'd made, I wished that I had taken more care in preparing the meal. It didn't look like much to set in front of company. But when we were all seated at the table, and Robert had said grace, no one seemed to mind.

"Robert, what did you want to see me about?" Gus asked. "It must be pretty important for you to walk to Jubilee."

Robert looked first at Mom, then he turned to Gus Tyson. "I wanted to know if you could use me at the sawmill, after school is out," Robert said. "I'll need a job for the summer."

This was the first I had heard of Robert wanting a job.

"Have you talked this over with your mother?"

Robert shook his head. "No, sir," he said. "I wanted to know if I could get a job before I asked Mom could I work."

Gus Tyson said, "Robert, talk to your mother about it. If it's all right with her, you've got a job at the sawmill. You could board with Fanny during the week." He added, "And we'd bring you home on Sunday."

Robert's face lit up like a thousand candles. He leaped from his chair, then he sat back down. "I sure do thank you," he told Gus.

"That's all right, son," Gus said quietly. "But don't let me hear tell of you worrying your mother, or running away again."

Robert sat real still, and his eyes got wide and innocent. "I wasn't going away forever, like Dustin Hollis," he said. "I was coming to see you. I'd have been home again before morning."

Gus Tyson nodded his head solemnly. "I see," he said. Then he turned to Mom. "Zel, if you could spare Robert on Saturdays, I could use him to help me in Oolitic for a few weeks."

When he left for Jubilee, it was all settled. Gus would come here for Robert every Saturday morning and bring him home at the end of the day.

All of a sudden, Robert seemed to stand ten feet tall. Even his voice sounded deeper. Mom said that it would be good for Robert to get out of the house and work with men. I didn't say so, but I thought that having Gus Tyson here tonight had already helped Robert.

I wasn't sure but what Gus Tyson's visit hadn't helped Mom also. When I mentioned going to see Fanny Phillips, Mom said, "No harm done, Seely. But the next time you want to see Fanny, you talk to me first."

It was later that night when I noticed the bare white band on Mom's finger, where her wide gold wedding band should have been.

She had her elbow on the table, her head resting in her cupped hand while she studied a page of figures, trying to find a budget we could live with. I thought she had gone to sleep. I was ready for bed, but I didn't want to leave her sleeping at the table.

"I was just resting my eyes," Mom said, when I touched her arm and reminded her of the time. "You go on to bed," she told me. "I'll be done here in a minute."

That's when I saw her bare finger. "Mom, where is your wedding ring? Have you lost it?"

She covered her left hand with her right. Then as if she realized it was too late to hide it, she spread both hands palm down on the table in front of her.

"I had to have the money for coal," Mom said quietly. "They wouldn't deliver it until after I had paid them."

Her eyes met mine squarely, with no regret or apology. "That ring couldn't keep us warm, Seely. But the money I borrowed on it will buy coal till after Easter."

"We could have managed somehow," I said. "It's not right that you should give up your wedding ring."

Mom smiled and reached out to me. "We couldn't have got through till spring, the way things were," she said. "Now we've got a chance."

I touched the bare spot on her finger, and Mom covered my hand with her own. "It isn't lost forever, Seely," she said softly. "I've got six months to redeem it. By that time, we won't need a fire to keep warm, and I'll have saved enough money to get my ring back."

chapter twenty-five

*T*hat night in January seemed to mark the end to one way of living and set the pattern for the days to come.

Gus Tyson would come to our house early on Saturday morning. He'd take Mom to work. Then he and Robert would go on to Oolitic to work on the house he had bought there. His car wouldn't be out of sight on Maple Street when Deidre would be at our house, knocking on the door. Deidre would pitch in and help me with the chores and by noon the wash would be on the line to dry and the day's work done.

Sometimes, we'd go to the Hollis farm and spend the

afternoon with Mersy Hollis. She hadn't heard a word from Dustin, she told me when I asked about him one day. She said she wasn't worried. He could take care of himself. Other times, we would walk downtown and window shop, or go to the movies. Grandpa Hollis had left a little money to Deidre, and she spent it freely for us to see a show. We always found time to go to Ray's Garage for a few minutes with Arlo Hawks. Or the Saturday he was bussing dishes at the hotel, we'd use the excuse we wanted to see Mom to talk to Arlo.

But no matter where we went, or what we did, I was always home in time to have supper ready to put on the table when Gus Tyson brought Mom and Robert home. Once in a while, Gus would stay to eat with us. But usually he would just wave to me and drive on home to Jubilee.

Robert came in covered with paint and plaster and full of stories about the house in Oolitic. To hear him tell it, not even Paul V. McNutt had a finer house. And he was the governor.

"You ought to see it," Robert told Mom.

Mom sniffed and turned away. "I've got better things to do with my time," she said shortly.

Sam Prophet had been down to our house again, threatening Mom with eviction if she didn't pay him the raise in the rent that he had asked for. He told Mom he needed the money for upkeep on the house.

Mom went to the hospital and paid Elvira Spragg the regular rent on the house.

"What Elvira does with the money afterwards is her

business," Mom said. "But I'll be switched if I'm going to give it to that man."

After Elvira Spragg came home from the hospital, Mom would go to the house to visit her. But whenever Robert and I stopped to see Mrs. Spragg, Sam Prophet told us that she was sleeping, and he wouldn't let us in. After that, Mom told Robert and me to stay away from the Spragg house and leave those people alone.

Robert and I used the alley beside the house weekdays going to school, and I used it on Saturdays, when Deidre and I went downtown. More times than not, after school Robert and I came back the long way round to the Hollises with Deidre.

While we were there, Robert carried firewood from the barn to the house and filled the woodbox for Mersy Hollis. Then he would clean the ashes from the stove and dump them. Mersy never mentioned Dustin's name, and we never brought it up. But when we were with Deidre we talked of Dustin, wondering where he was and what he was doing.

One evening, as we were leaving, Robert said, "Mrs. Hollis, I'll bring Dustin's sled home tomorrow. You might need it."

Mersy smiled at Robert and put her hand on his arm. "You keep that sled, Robert. Dustin wanted you to have it, or he wouldn't have left it with you."

In all the time we spent with Mersy Hollis that was the only time I heard her speak of Dustin. She didn't talk about Grandpa Hollis either. It was as though she was trying to forget that he had ever been here.

* * *

The last week of March brought a warm spell to southern Indiana. By the first Saturday in April, we were wearing only sweaters, or no wraps at all. Deidre came to the house about nine o'clock that morning, but she hadn't come to help me with the chores. That was plain to see. She had on the clothes she had bought for graduation three weeks from now, and she carried a coat over her arm.

I had never seen Deidre dressed so fine, with her hair smoothed back from her face. I felt like she had grown much older overnight, and now I didn't know her.

"Well?" Deidre twirled around for my inspection. "How do I look?"

"You look fine," I said. "But you won't need that coat today."

"I might need it later," Deidre said. She moved uneasily about the room, then came to rest near me. "Seely, Arlo is leaving for Michigan this morning, and I'm going with him."

"Couldn't Arlo wait till your graduation and then go north?" I asked. "It's only three weeks."

Deidre shook her head. "He can't wait," she said. "He has this job in Detroit, and he is supposed to be at work the first of the week."

We stood looking at each other in an uncomfortable silence, Deidre anxious to be on her way to meet Arlo Hawks, yet not knowing how to leave gracefully. And I wondered how she could even consider leaving here at this time.

Finally, Deidre smiled and reached for me. "I've got to go, Seely. Wish me luck."

She held me close for a moment, then she turned and ran.

I said, "Oh, Deidre, I do wish you luck. I wish you happy." But she never heard me. The words were a whisper, spoken to an empty room.

chapter twenty-six

I hadn't done housework in the Spragg house since Mrs. Spragg had broken her hip, and my other jobs were only occasional. My hands were all healed and not a scar showed to remind me of what had been. When I got word that old Miss Wade needed help with her spring house cleaning, I didn't hesitate for a minute. I said I would do it.

On the way to school on Monday, I told Robert not to wait for me after school. I'd be working for Miss Wade, and I didn't know what time I would get home.

Robert said, "Is it all right if I go to Mrs. Hollis's for a while?"

I said that he could go. "But you be home before dark," I added.

I hadn't told Mom or Robert that Deidre had said she was going to Michigan with Arlo Hawks on Saturday. I thought there would be time enough to talk about it, when I knew for sure she had gone. Now, Robert would find out from Mersy Hollis what had happened.

It was after dark when I got home from the Wade place. Mom and Robert were both there before me. They had been home long enough to build a fire in the cookstove and make hamburgers and biscuits for our supper.

Mom said, "Seely, you know I don't like you being out after dark."

I tossed my sweater toward a chair and went to wash my hands. "I wanted to get done today," I said, "so I wouldn't have to go back tomorrow."

"Should anyone else ask," Mom said, "you tell them you can't work until school is out. I won't have you walking the streets alone in the dark," she added.

We sat down at the table to eat. The sandwich and apple that I'd had for lunch was wearing very thin by now and I was hungry.

"I guess it's no news to you," Mom went on, "that Deidre Hollis married Arlo Hawks on Saturday and they've gone to live in Michigan."

I choked on a bite of biscuit and hamburger.

"Deidre married Arlo Hawks?" I asked, when I got my wind back.

"The marriage license notice was in today's paper," Mom answered. "And it gave Arlo's address as Detroit, Michigan."

193

"Mrs. Hollis was packing Deidre's things while I was there," Robert said, eager to add what he knew. "She told me that Deidre would send for them."

"It won't be easy for Arlo and Deidre," Mom said. "But they are young. They will make it all right. Pulling up stakes and moving to a strange place is a lot harder as you grow older."

I knew she was referring to our move to Bedford. Mom had never come right out and said that she regretted it. And she had never wished to go back. But I'd heard her say once that she'd had a taste of daylight now, and she didn't like it. I couldn't say that I liked living in the city either. But I had never expected to like it.

Robert went to see Mrs. Hollis whenever he could, but I only saw her one time after Deidre went away.

It was Mom's payday and she had asked Robert and me to come to the hotel when we got out of school. As we passed the bus station, we saw Mersy Hollis standing outside the door. "Waiting for the southbound bus," Mersy told us with a wide smile. She had heard from Dustin, and she was on her way to join him in Georgia.

"If I like it down there," she said, "I'll be back to sell the farm and move to Georgia for good. Dustin says it's a good, warm country down there, with plain folks just like ourselves for neighbors."

Robert and I waited with Mersy Hollis and walked to the bus door with her as she was leaving. We waved to her until the bus turned the corner and went out of sight. Then we went on to the hotel to meet Mom.

194

"It's just as well that I'll be working in Jubilee this summer," Robert said. "I've no friends left here."

I wondered how I would get through the summer. I was seventeen years old. I knew the names of everyone in my class at school, yet I didn't have one close friend among them. And I couldn't expect to meet anyone my age while I was cleaning houses for elderly women.

It was a quiet trio who shopped for groceries that afternoon and carried them home later.

Mom had seemed pleased to hear that Mersy Hollis was going to Georgia to visit Dustin and perhaps to move there for good. She said she was happy as could be for them both. But now her mind seemed a million miles away from Mersy, Dustin, and Robert and me as she stepped off the blocks toward home. For once, Robert didn't have anything to say. And I kept my thoughts to myself.

Later that night, Mom came from her room with a letter. I could tell it had been read many times. The writing was almost worn off the envelope.

"I had this letter from Julie the other day," Mom said, "and now that school is about over, I want you to hear what she has to say."

She started reading the letter aloud to Robert and me. "You asked could I take Seely in to live with me," Julie wrote. "I would like it very much. She could work with me during the summer at the library and finish school up here."

Mom stopped reading and folded the letter. She looked at me for a long moment, then she said, "Seely, it is up to you. Would you like to live with Julie and go to school there?"

I had dreamed of the day when I could live with Julie and learn to be a lady, the way she was. But I knew this wasn't the time.

"I'd like that more than anything in the world," I said. "And maybe next year I can do that. But I can't go now. There would be no one here with you this summer, and no one to stay with Robert while you work next winter."

"Seely, you can argue your life away like that," Mom said. "You'd never have what you want. You say you'd like to go to live with Julie, then you should go. I'll write her to expect you as soon as school is out this next week," she added.

As if it was all settled, Mom took Julie's letter and went to her room to answer it.

I looked at Robert, sitting there wide-eyed and quiet. He had grown as tall as I was, and at times he seemed to be as old. But this wasn't one of those times.

"You'll go away, and I'll never see you again," he said.

I sat down beside Robert. He had been like my shadow these past months. I didn't want to leave him. Yet I didn't want to give up what living with Julie promised me either. Why did I have to give up one, I thought, to have the other?

"Robert, I'm not going anywhere," I said, "until I find out why Mom wrote and asked Julie to take me. It's clear that Mom did write Julie. Julie would never have written like this otherwise."

"You'll go," he said.

"Even if I did, I'd always come back to see you," I assured him.

Robert didn't say a word. He just sat there and shook his head no. There didn't seem to be anything for either one of us to say.

chapter twenty-seven

Gus and Fanny are coming this morning to take us to Oolitic to see that house Gus has been working on," Mom said. "Seely, you and Robert get dressed while I clear the table." She gathered up our few breakfast dishes and put them in the sink.

Mom had said that it was almost too warm this Sunday to make a breakfast fire. But she hadn't yet learned to live without her morning coffee. We had dry cereal for breakfast, and as soon as the coffee perked the fire was allowed to die.

Robert said, "Are you really going to look at the house?"

Mom smiled at Robert. "Nothing else would do Gus Tyson but take Seely and me to see what you've been doing. This is the only chance we'll have to see it before Seely goes up north to live with your sister."

Ever since the night it had been settled to Mom's satisfaction that I would go to live with Julie, she seemed to begin and end everything she said with "when Seely goes north."

One minute I was excited and eager to be on my way. Then I would be scared to death at the thought of leaving home and everything I was used to here.

"Seely, stop your dreaming and get dressed," Mom said. "They'll be here any minute."

I went to change my clothes.

The house in Oolitic was everything Robert had said it was and much more. He hadn't told us about the high stained-glass windows that lighted the wide stairway and turned the plain carpet into a kaleidoscope of colors. He hadn't said a word about the kitchen either, with the solid wall of cabinets and a gas range and refrigerator. I touched the smooth wood of the cabinets and ran my hand across the workbench.

"It just about takes your breath away, don't it, Seely?"

I hadn't heard Robert come in. I'd thought he was with Gus, or Mom and Fanny, in another part of the house.

"Can you imagine living in a place like this?" I spoke in the same low tone that Robert had used. "Fanny Phillips won't know what to do with herself in a kitchen like this one," I added.

199

"There is a furnace in the basement," Robert said, "a washing machine, and lines to dry the clothes on when it rains."

We marveled at the conveniences that Fanny would have at her fingertips. Things she had probably never dared to hope for, I told Robert.

We had looked the place over inside and out, when Mom called that it was time to go.

Gus Tyson took us all to dinner at a restaurant in Bedford, then he drove us back home.

Gus and Fanny came in long enough for Fanny to trim Robert's hair, so it would be neat for the last day of school. Then she threatened to cut mine if I didn't do something with it.

She touched her short-bobbed salt and pepper hair. "If I had that mop of long heavy hair, I'd take the scissors to it," she said. "I don't know how you stand it."

Gus Tyson smiled at me. "Seely, pay no mind to her preaching," he said. "Fanny is apt to get scissor-happy at times."

Fanny Phillips snorted and put Mom's shears back on the shelf.

At the door, as they were leaving, Gus turned to Mom. "Zel, I'll talk to you tomorrow."

Mom just nodded her head.

Later that night, Mom sat down at the table beside Robert. Then she called me to come sit with them. "I want to talk to you kids," she said.

I sat down. But it took a while for Mom to say anything. Finally, she took a deep breath and looked straight at me, as if I was the one who would decide the outcome of this talk.

"Seely, I'm of a mind to marry Gus Tyson," Mom said, "and live with him in that house in Oolitic."

Robert said, "Are you joking us?"

"If that is a joke," I said, "it's not funny."

Mom looked at Robert, then at me. "I was never more serious," she said.

I shoved my chair away from the table and started toward the loft room.

"Seely," Mom said. "Come here. I'm not through talking to you."

"What else is there to say?"

I waited for a moment. When Mom didn't order me back to the table, I went on to my room.

Now I knew why Mom had asked Julie to take me off her hands, I thought. She had known all the while that she was going to marry Gus Tyson as soon as that house was finished. But she hadn't said a word until she knew for sure that I wouldn't be here. I threw myself onto my bed and closed my eyes.

I heard the creak of the steps as someone came up to my room. I lay still, as if I was asleep. I couldn't comfort myself tonight, I thought, let alone Robert.

A hand touched me. Then Mom sat down on the side of my bed beside me.

"Hear me out, Seely. Before you raise any questions," she said quietly.

I didn't move or say a word.

"I'm fond of Gus," Mom began. "He's a good steady

man. And Robert is at the age where he needs a man's guidance."

Mom paused, and I felt her hand smoothing my hair back from my face, touching me tenderly. As if she thought to make me understand through her touch.

"Robert will soon be grown," Mom said softly. "You will have your own life. Seely, I need a life for myself. I've no desire to grow old alone," she added.

"Is that why you wrote to Julie? You wanted me out of the house, so you could marry Gus Tyson?"

Mom got still as death. I thought she wasn't going to answer me. Then she let her breath out in a long sigh.

"Seely, the thought of marrying Gus had never entered my mind when I wrote to Julie," Mom said. "I wrote to Julie hoping that I could make your life easier for you than it has been.

"Night after night, I sat in my room and watched you up here, always writing in that little book of yours. I wondered what you found to write about. One day I came across the book downstairs, where you had forgotten and left it. As soon as I opened it, I saw it was your diary. But I read the page where it opened to. You had written that as soon as Robert didn't need you, you would go to live with Julie.

"I put the diary back where I'd found it. But it started me to thinking. Robert would be working at the sawmill, boarding all week with Fanny. There'd be no need for you to stay on his account. I figured you could use this time for something better than cleaning after other people. That's when I wrote to Julie," she added. "Told her what I had in mind for you."

"I'm scared to go up there to live," I said. "I won't know how to act around those people."

"Maybe not at first," Mom said. "But by the time school starts, Julie will have you looking and acting just like her."

Mom got off the bed and started toward the steps, hugging the wall away from the balcony.

"This is the first time you've ever been in my room," I said.

Mom kind of laughed and turned to back down the steps. "Seely, don't you know by now that your mother is scared to death of heights?"

Mom married Gus Tyson at ten o'clock the next Sunday morning. Fanny Phillips and Robert and I stood up with them in the parlor of the Justice of the Peace. When Gus slipped the ring on Mom's finger, there was no sign of the white band where Dad's ring had been.

We went straight from the Justice of the Peace to the bus station, where I would take the northbound bus to Julie. Gus Tyson got my ticket and carried my bag to the waiting bus, while I said my goodbyes to Mom and Robert.

It wasn't easy. I said, "I'll see you, little brother," to Robert's quiet, wide-eyed look. Then I turned to Mom.

Mom hugged me so tight, I couldn't breathe. I said, "Mom!" She stepped back and gave me a little push.

"Go on, now," she said. "And behave yourself!"

Gus Tyson was standing at the door of the bus to help me aboard. "If you need anything . . ."

"I know," I said quickly.

203

He shoved a small wrapped package into my hand, then turned and hurried away.

When we had left the city behind, and there was only the open road ahead, I opened the package Gus had given me. I lifted the lid of the jeweler's box it held and took the fine gold chain and wide wedding band in my hand.

Inscribed inside the wedding band were Mom's and Dad's initials and the words, "Love without end." I closed my hand tight around the ring and held it close to me.

Dad had given this ring to Mom. Now Gus Tyson had given it to me for safe-keeping. I was leaving home, but I was taking with me the token of Mom's and Dad's love. And their love for me.

Love without end, the inscription read. I had never heard either of them use the word love to each other. But their care and concern had taught us its meaning.

"Miss, are you all right?"

My face was wet with tears, but I smiled at the elderly lady who had spoken and nodded my head.

"I'm fine," I said. "I always cry when I'm happy."

I turned to the window and watched as the world came racing to meet me and, as quickly, rushed on by.

AUTHOR'S NOTE

With the publication of *A Taste of Daylight*, the fifth and final book about the Robinson family of Greene County, Indiana, I would like to thank the libraries, schools, and general public for the wide acclaim they have given these books.

Many people who have read about Seely Robinson and her family believe the stories to be true. I have received thousands of letters inquiring about Julie and Robert, and their mother, Zel. One kind and caring person wrote from Greene County and asked where my brother Jamie was buried and offered to care for his grave. To these people I offer my heartfelt gratitude for the compliment they have paid to me. As an author, I had hoped that my work would be believable, but I never dreamed it would be so believable.

A few of the towns and the country roads in my books can be found on the map of Indiana. But the people and events I depict are strictly fictional.

Crystal Thrasher
Roanoke, Indiana
January 20, 1984